The Nutcracker and Mouse King

By

E. T. A. Hoffmann

British Library Cataloguing-in-Publication Data
A catalogue record for this book is available from the
British Library

Contents

E. T. A. Hoffman   4

CHRISTMAS EVE   7
THE CHRISTMAS PRESENTS.   11
MARIE'S PET AND PROTÉGEÉ.   16
WONDERFUL EVENTS.   21
THE BATTLE.   32
THE INVALID.   38
THE STORY OF THE HARD NUT.   43
UNCLE AND NEPHEW.   64
VICTORY.   68
THE METROPOLIS.   82

CONCLUSION.   91

E. T. A. Hoffman

Ernst Theodor Wilhelm Hoffmann was born in Königsberg, East Prussia in 1776. His family were all jurists, and during his youth he was initially encouraged to pursue a career in law. However, in his late teens Hoffman became increasingly interested in literature and philosophy, and spent much of his time reading German classicists and attending lectures by, amongst others, Immanuel Kant.

In was in his twenties, upon moving with his uncle to Berlin, that Hoffman first began to promote himself as a composer, writing an operetta called Die Maske and entering a number of playwriting competitions. Hoffman struggled to establish himself anywhere for a while, flitting between a number of cities and dodging the attentions of Napoleon's occupying troops. In 1808, while living in Bamberg, he began his job as a theatre manager and a music critic, and Hoffman's break came a year later, with the publication of Ritter Gluck. The story centred on a man who meets, or thinks he has met, a long-dead composer, and played into the 'doppelgänger' theme – at that time very popular in literature. It was shortly after this that Hoffman began to use the pseudonym E. T. A. Hoffmann, declaring the 'A' to stand for 'Amadeus', as a tribute to the great composer, Mozart.

Over the next decade, while moving between Dresden, Leipzig and Berlin, Hoffman produced a great range of both literary and musical works. Probably Hoffman's most well-known story, produced in 1816, is 'The Nutcracker and the Mouse King', due to the fact that – some seventy-six years later - it inspired Tchaikovsky's ballet The Nutcracker.

In the same vein, his story 'The Sandman' provided both the inspiration for Léo Delibes's ballet Coppélia, and the basis for a highly influential essay by Sigmund Freud, called 'The Uncanny'. (Indeed, Freud referred to Hoffman as the "unrivalled master of the uncanny in literature.")

Alcohol abuse and syphilis eventually took a great toll on Hoffman though, and – having spent the last year of his life paralysed – he died in Berlin in 1822, aged just 46. His legacy is a powerful one, however: He is seen as a pioneer of both Romanticism and fantasy literature, and his novella, Mademoiselle de Scudéri: A Tale from the Times of Louis XIV is often cited as the first ever detective story.

CHRISTMAS EVE

"**On** the 24th of December Dr. Stahlbaum's children were not allowed, on any pretext whatever, at any time of all that day, to go into the small drawing-room, much less into the best drawing-room into which it opened. Fritz and Marie were sitting cowered together in a corner of the back parlour when the evening twilight fell, and they began to feel terribly eery. Seeing that no candles were brought, as was generally the case on Christmas Eve, Fritz, whispering in a mysterious fashion, confided to his young sister (who was just seven) that he had heard rattlings and rustlings going on all day, since early morning, inside the forbidden rooms, as well as distant hammerings. Further, that a short time ago a little dark-looking man had gone slipping and creeping across the floor with a big box under his arm, though he was well aware that this little man was no other than Godpapa Drosselmeier. At this news Marie clapped her little hands for gladness, and cried:

Oh! I do wonder what pretty things Godpapa Drosselmeier has been making for us this time!'

"Godpapa Drosselmeier was anything but a nice-looking man. He was little and lean, with a great many wrinkles on his face, a big patch of black plaister where his right eye ought to have been, and not a hair on his head; which was why he wore a fine white wig, made of glass, and a very beautiful work of art. But he was a very, very clever man, who even knew and understood all about clocks and watches, and could make them himself. So that when one of the beautiful clocks that were in Dr. Stahlbaum's house was out of sorts, and couldn't sing, Godpapa Drosselmeier would come, take off his glass periwig and his little yellow coat, gird himself with a blue apron, and proceed to stick sharp-pointed instruments into the inside of the clock, in a way that made little Marie quite miserable to witness. However, this didn't really hurt the poor clock, which, on the contrary, would come to life again, and begin to whirr and sing and strike as merrily as ever; which caused everybody the greatest satisfaction. Of course, whenever he came he always brought something delightful in his pockets for the children--perhaps a little man, who would roll his eyes and make bows and scrapes, most comic to behold; or a box, out of which a little bird would jump; or something else of the kind. But for Christmas he always had some specially charming piece of ingenuity provided; something which had cost him infinite pains and labour-- for which reason it was always taken away and put by with the greatest care by the children's parents.

Oh! what can Godpapa Drosselmeier have been making for us this time.' Marie cried, as we have said.

"Fritz was of opinion that, this time, it could hardly be anything but a great castle, a fortress, where all sorts of pretty soldiers would be drilling and marching about; and then, that other soldiers would come and try to get into the fortress, upon which the soldiers inside would fire away at them, as pluckily as you please, with cannon, till every thing banged and thundered like anything.

No, no,' Marie said. 'Godpapa Drosselmeier once told me about a beautiful garden, with a great lake in it, and beautiful swans swimming about with great gold collars, singing lovely music. And then a lovely little girl comes down through the garden to the lake, and calls the swans and feeds them with shortbread and cake.'

Swans don't eat cake and shortbread,' Fritz cried, rather rudely (with masculine superiority); 'and Godpapa Drosselmeier couldn't make a whole garden. After all, we have got very few of his playthings; whatever he brings is always taken away from us. So I like the things papa and mamma give us much better; we keep them, all right, ourselves, and can do what we like with them.'

"The children went on discussing as to what he might have in store for them this time. Marie called Fritz's attention to the fact that Miss Gertrude (her biggest doll) appeared to be failing a good deal as time went on, inasmuch as she was more clumsy and awkward than ever, tumbling on to the floor every two or three minutes, a thing which did not occur without leaving very ugly marks on her face, and of course a proper condition of her clothes became out of the question altogether. Scolding was of no use. Mamma too had laughed at her for being so delighted with Miss Gertrude's little new parasol. Fritz, again, remarked that a good fox was lacking to his small zoological collection, and that his army was quite without cavalry, as his papa was well aware. But the children knew that their elders had got all sorts of charming things ready for them, as also that the Child-Christ, at Christmas time, took special care for their wants. Marie sat in thoughtful silence, but Fritz murmured quietly to himself:

All the same, I should like a fox and some hussars!'

"It was now quite dark; Fritz and Marie sitting close together, did not dare to utter another syllable; they felt as if there were a fluttering of gentle, invisible wings around them, whilst a very far away, but unutterably beautiful strain of music could dimly be heard. Then a bright gleam of light passed quickly athwart the wall, and the children knew that the Child-Christ had sped away, on shining wings, to other happy children. At this moment a silvery bell said, 'Kling-ling! Kling-ling!' the doors flew open, and such a brilliance of light came streaming from the drawing-room that the children stood rooted where they were with cries of 'Oh! Oh!'

"But papa and mamma came and took their hands, saying, 'Come now, darlings, and see what the blessed Child-Christ has brought for you.'

THE CHRISTMAS PRESENTS.

"I appeal to yourself, kind reader (or listener)--Fritz, Theodore, Ernest, or whatsoever your name may chance to be--and I would beg you to bring vividly before your mind's eye your last Christmas table, all glorious with its various delightful Christmas presents; and then perhaps you will be able to form some idea of the manner in which the two children stood speechless with brilliant glances fixed on all the beautiful things; how, after a little, Marie, with a sigh, cried, 'Oh, how lovely! how lovely!' and Fritz gave several jumps of delight. The children had certainly been very, very good and well-behaved all the foregoing year to be thus rewarded; for never had so many beautiful and delightful things been provided for them as this time. The great Christmas tree on the table bore many apples of silver and gold, and all its branches were heavy with bud and blossom, consisting of sugar almonds, many-tinted bonbons, and all sorts of charming things to eat. Perhaps the prettiest thing about this wonder-tree, however, was the fact that in all the recesses of its spreading branches hundreds of little tapers glittered like stars, inviting the children to pluck its flowers and fruit. Also, all round the tree on every side everything shone and glittered in the loveliest manner. Oh, how many beautiful things there were! Who, oh who, could describe them all? Marie gazed there at the most delicious dolls, and all kinds of toys, and (what was the prettiest thing of all) a little silk dress with many-tinted ribbons was hung upon a projecting branch in such sort that she could admire it on all its sides; which she accordingly did, crying out several times, 'Oh! the lovely, the lovely, darling little dress. And I suppose, I do believe, I shall really be allowed to put it on!' Fritz, in the meantime, had had two or three trials how his new fox (which he had actually found on the table) could gallop; and now stated that he seemed a wildish sort of brute; but, no matter, he felt sure he would soon get him well in order; and he set to work to muster his new squadron of hussars, admirably equipped, in red and gold uniforms, with real silver swords, and mounted on such shining white horses that you would have thought they were of pure silver too.

"When the children had sobered down a little, and were beginning upon the beautiful picture books (which were open, so that you could see all sorts of most beautiful flowers and people of every hue, to say nothing of lovely children playing, all as naturally represented as if they were really alive and could speak), there came another tinkling of a bell, to announce the display of Godpapa Drosselmeier's Christmas present, which was on another table, against the wall, concealed by a curtain. When this curtain was drawn, what did the children behold?

"On a green lawn, bright with flowers, stood a lordly castle with a great many shining windows and golden towers. A chime of bells was going on inside it; doors and windows opened, and you saw very small, but beautiful, ladies and gentlemen, with plumed hats, and long robes down to their heels, walking up and down in the rooms of it. In the central hall, which seemed all in a blaze, there were quantities of little candles burning in silver chandeliers; children, in little short doublets, were dancing to the chimes of the bells. A gentleman, in an emerald green mantle, came to a window, made signs thereat, and then disappeared inside again; also, even Godpapa Drosselmeier himself (but scarcely taller than papa's thumb) came now and then, and stood at the castle door, then went in again.

"Fritz had been looking on with the rest at the beautiful castle and the people walking about and dancing in it, with his arms leant on the table; then he said:

Godpapa Drosselmeier, let me go into your castle for a little.'

"Drosselmeier answered that this could not possibly be done. In which he was right; for it was silly of Fritz to want to go into a castle which was not so tall as himself, golden towers and all. And Fritz saw that this was so.

"After a short time, as the ladies and gentlemen kept on walking about just in the same fashion, the children dancing, and the emerald man looking out at the same window, and God papa Drosselmeier coming to the door Fritz cried impatiently:

Godpapa Drosselmeier, please come out at that other door!'

That can't be done, dear Fritz,' answered Drosselmeier.

Well,' resumed Fritz, 'make that green man that looks out so often walk about with the others.'

And that can't be done, either,' said his godpapa, once

more.

Make the children come down, then,' said Fritz. 'I want to see them nearer.'

Nonsense, nothing of that sort can be done,' cried Drosselmeier, with impatience. 'The machinery must work as it's doing now; it can't be altered, you know.'

"Oh,' said Fritz, 'it can't be done, eh? Very well, then, Godpapa Drosselmeier, I'll tell you what it is. If your little creatures in the castle there can only always do the same thing, they're not much worth, and I think precious little of them! No, give me my hussars. They've got to manœuvre backwards and forwards just as I want them, and are not fastened up in a house.'

"With which he made off to the other table, and set his squadron of silver horse trotting here and there, wheeling and charging and slashing right and left to his heart's content. Marie had slipped away softly, too, for she was tired of the promenading and dancing of the puppets in the castle, though, kind and gentle as she was, she did not like to show it as her brother did. Drosselmeier, somewhat annoyed, said to the parents--'After all, an ingenious piece of mechanism like this is not a matter for children, who don't understand it; I shall put my castle back in its box again.' But the mother came to the rescue, and made him show her the clever machinery which moved the figures, Drosselmeier taking it all to pieces, putting it together again, and quite recovering his temper in the process. So that he gave the children all sorts of delightful brown men and women with golden faces, hands and legs, which were made of ginger cake, and with which they were greatly content.

MARIE'S PET AND PROTÉGÉE.

"But there was a reason wherefore Marie found it against the grain to come away from the table where the Christmas presents were laid out; and this was, that she had just noticed a something there which she had not observed at first. Fritz's hussars having taken ground to the right at some distance from the tree, in front of which they had previously been paraded, there became visible a most delicious little man, who was standing there quiet and unobtrusive, as if waiting patiently till it should be his turn to be noticed. Objection, considerable objection, might, perhaps, have been taken to him on the score of his figure, for his body was rather too tall and stout for his legs, which were short and slight; moreover, his head was a good deal too large. But much of this was atoned for by the elegance of his costume, which showed him to be a person of taste and cultivation. He had on a very pretty violet hussar's jacket, all over knobs and braiding, pantaloons of the same, and the loveliest little boots ever seen even on a hussar officer--fitting his dear little legs just as if they had been painted on to them. It was funny, certainly, that, dressed in this style as he was, he had on a little, rather absurd, short cloak on his shoulders, which looked almost as if it were made of wood, and on his head a cap like a miner's. But Marie remembered that Godpapa Drosselmeier often appeared in a terribly ugly morning jacket, and with a frightful looking cap on his head, and yet was a very very darling godpapa.

"As Marie kept looking at this little man, whom she had quite fallen in love with at first sight, she saw more and more clearly what a sweet nature and disposition was legible in his countenance. Those green eyes of his (which stuck, perhaps, a little more prominently out of his head than was quite desirable) beamed with kindliness and benevolence. It was one of his beauties, too, that his chin was set off with a well kept beard of white cotton, as this drew attention to the sweet smile which his bright red lips always expressed.

Oh, papa, dear!' cried Marie at last, 'whose is that most darling little man beside the tree?'

"Well,' was the answer, 'that little fellow is going to do plenty of good service for all of you; he's going to crack nuts for you, and he is to belong to Louise just as much as to you and Fritz.' With which papa took him up from the table, and on his lifting the end of his wooden cloak, the little man opened his mouth wider and wider, displaying two rows of very white, sharp teeth. Marie, directed by her father, put a nut into his mouth, and--knack--he had bitten it in two, so that the shells fell down, and Marie got the kernel. So then it was explained to all that this charming little man belonged to the Nutcracker family, and was practising the profession of his ancestors. 'And,' said papa, 'as friend Nutcracker seems to have made such an impression on you, Marie, he shall be given over to your special care and charge, though, as I said, Louise and Fritz are to have the same right to his services as you.'

"Marie took him into her arms at once, and made him

crack some more nuts; but she picked out all the smallest, so that he might not have to open his mouth so terribly wide, because that was not nice for him. Then sister Louise came, and he had to crack some nuts for her too,' which duty he seemed very glad to perform, as he kept on smiling most courteously.

"Meanwhile, Fritz was a little tired, after so much drill and manœuvring, so he joined his sisters, and laughed beyond measure at the funny little fellow, who (as Fritz wanted his share of the nuts) was passed from hand to hand, and was continually snapping his month open and shut. Fritz gave him all the biggest and hardest nuts he could find, but all at once there was a 'crack--crack,' and three teeth fell out of Nutcracker's mouth, and all his lower jaw was loose and wobbly.

Ah! my poor darling Nutcracker,' Marie cried, and took him away from Fritz.

A nice sort of chap he is!' said Fritz. 'Calls himself a nutcracker, and can't give a decent bite--doesn't seem to know much about his business. Hand him over here, Marie! I'll keep him biting nuts if he drops all the rest of his teeth, and his jaw into the bargain. What's the good of a chap like him!'

No, no,' said Marie, in tears; 'you shan't have him, my darling Nutcracker; see how he's looking at me so mournfully, and showing me his poor sore mouth. But you're a hard-hearted creature! You beat your horses, and you've had one of your soldiers shot.'

18

Those things must be done,' said Fritz; 'and you don't understand anything about such matters. But Nutcracker's as much mine as yours, so hand him over!'

"Marie began to cry bitterly, and wrapped the wounded Nutcracker quickly up in her little pocket-handkerchief. Papa and mamma came with Drosselmeier, who took Fritz's part, to Marie's regret. But papa said, 'I have put Nutcracker in Marie's special charge, and as he seems to have need just now of her care, she has full power over him, and nobody else has anything to say in the matter. And I'm surprised that Fritz should expect further service from a man wounded in the execution of his duty. As a good soldier, he ought to know better than that.'

"Fritz was much ashamed, and, troubling himself no further as to nuts or nutcrackers, crept off to the other side of the table, where his hussars (having established the necessary outposts and videttes) were bivouacking for the night. Marie got Nutcracker's lost teeth together, bound a pretty white ribbon, taken from her dress, about his poor chin, and then wrapped the poor little fellow, who was looking very pale and frightened, more tenderly and carefully than before in her handkerchief. Thus she held him, rocking him like a child in her arms, as she looked at the picture-books. She grew quite angry (which was not usual with her) with Godpapa Drosselmeier because he laughed so, and kept asking how she could make such a fuss about an ugly little fellow like that. That odd and peculiar likeness to Drosselmeier, which had struck her when she saw Nutcracker at first, occurred to her mind again now, and she said, with much earnestness:

Who knows, godpapa, if you were to be dressed the same as my darling Nutcracker, and had on the same shining boots--who knows whether you mightn't look almost as handsome as he does?'

"Marie did not understand why papa and mamma laughed so heartily, nor why Godpapa Drosselmeier's nose got so red, nor why he did not join so much in the laughter as before. Probably there was some special reason for these things.

WONDERFUL EVENTS.

"We must now explain that, in the sitting-room, on the left-hand as you go in, there stands, against the wall, a high, glass-fronted cupboard, where all the children's Christmas presents are yearly put away to be kept. Louise, the elder sister, was still quite little when her father had this cupboard constructed by a very skilful workman, who had put in it such transparent panes of glass, and altogether made the whole affair so splendid, that the things, when inside it, looked almost more shining and lovely than when one had them actually in one's hands. In the upper shelves, which were beyond the reach of Fritz and Marie, were stowed Godpapa Drosselmeier's works of art; immediately under them was the shelf for the picture-books. Fritz and Marie were allowed to do what they liked with the two lower shelves, but it always came about that the lower one of all was that in which Marie put away her dolls, as their place of residence, whilst Fritz utilized the shelf above this as cantonments for his troops of all arms. So that, on the evening as to which we are speaking, Fritz had quartered his hussars in his-- the upper--shelf of these two, whilst Marie had put Miss Gertrude rather in a corner, established her new doll in the well-appointed chamber there, with all its appropriate furniture, and invited herself to tea and cakes with her. This chamber was splendidly furnished, everything on a first-rate scale, and in good and admirable style, as I have already said--and I don't know if you, my observant reader, have the satisfaction of possessing an equally well-appointed room for your dolls; a little beautifully-flowered sofa, a number of the most charming little chairs, a nice little tea-table, and, above all, a beautiful little white bed, where your pretty darlings of dolls go to sleep? All this was in a corner of the shelf, the walls of which, in this part, had beautiful little pictures hanging on them; and you may well imagine that, in such a delightful chamber as this, the new doll (whose name, as Marie had discovered, was Miss Clara) thought herself extremely comfortably settled, and remarkably well off.

"It was getting very late, not so very far from midnight, indeed, before the children could tear themselves away from all these Yuletide fascinations, and Godpapa Drosselmeier had been gone a considerable time. They remained riveted beside the glass cupboard, although their mother several times reminded them that it was long after bedtime. 'Yes,' said Fritz, 'I know well enough that these poor fellows (meaning his hussars) are tired enough, and awfully anxious to turn in for the night, though as long as I'm here, not a man-jack of them dares to nod his head.' With which he went off. But Marie earnestly begged for just a little while longer, saying she had such a number of things to see to, and promising that as soon as ever she had got them all settled she would go to bed at once. Marie was a very good and reasonable child, and therefore her mother allowed her to remain for a little longer with her toys; but lest she should be too much occupied with her new doll and the other playthings so as to forget to put out the candles which were lighted all round on the wall sconces, she herself put all of them out, leaving merely the lamp which hung from the ceiling to give a soft and pleasant light. 'Come soon to your bed, Marie, or you'll never be up in time in the morning,' cried her mother as she went away into the bedroom.

"As soon as Marie was alone, she set rapidly to work to do the thing which was chiefly at her heart to accomplish, and which, though she scarcely knew why, she somehow did not like to set about in her mother's presence. She had been holding Nutcracker, wrapped in the handkerchief, carefully in her arms all this time, and she now laid him softly down on the table, gently unrolled the handkerchief, and examined his wounds.

"Nutcracker was very pale, but at the same time he was smiling with a melancholy and pathetic kindliness which went straight to Marie's heart.

"Oh, my darling little Nutcracker!' said she, very softly, 'don't you be vexed because brother Fritz has hurt you so: he didn't mean it, you know; he's only a little bit hardened with his soldiering and that, but he's a good, nice boy, I can assure you: and I'll take the greatest care of you, and nurse you, till you're quite, quite better and happy again. And your teeth shall be put in again for you, and your shoulder set right; Godpapa Drosselmeier will see to that; he knows how to do things of the kind----'

"Marie could not finish what she was going to say, because at the mention of Godpapa Drosselmeier, friend Nutcracker made a most horrible, ugly face. A sort of green sparkle of much sharpness seemed to dart out of his eyes. This was only for an instant, however; and just as Marie was going to be terribly frightened, she found that she was looking at the very same nice, kindly face, with the pathetic smile which she had seen before, and she saw plainly that it was nothing but some draught of air making the lamp flicker that had seemed to produce the change.

Well!' she said, 'I certainly am a silly girl to be so easily frightened, and think that a wooden doll could make faces at me! But I'm too fond, really, of Nutcracker, because he's so funny, and so kind and nice; and so he must be taken the greatest care of, and properly nursed till he's quite well.'

"With which she took him in her arms again, approached the cupboard, and kneeling down beside it, said to her new doll:

"I'm going to ask a favour of you, Miss Clara--that you will give up your bed to this poor sick, wounded Nutcracker, and make yourself as comfortable as you can on the sofa here. Remember that you're quite well and strong yourself, or you wouldn't have such fat, red cheeks, and that there are very few dolls indeed who have as comfortable a sofa as this to lie upon.'

"Miss Clara, in her Christmas full dress, looked very grand and disdainful, and said not so much as 'Muck!'

"Very well,' said Marie, 'why should I make such a fuss, and stand on any ceremony?'--took the bed and moved it forward; laid Nutcracker carefully and tenderly down on it; wrapped another pretty ribbon, taken from her own dress, about his hurt shoulder, and drew the bed-clothes up to his nose.

"But he shan't stay with that nasty Clara,' she said, and moved the bed, with Nutcracker in it, up to the upper shelf, so that it was placed near the village in which Fritz's hussars had their cantonments. She closed the cupboard, and was moving away to go to bed, when--listen, children! there begun a low soft rustling and rattling, and a sort of whispering noise, all round, in all directions, from all quarters of the room--behind the stove, under the chairs, behind the cupboards. The clock on the wall 'warned' louder and louder, but could not strike. Marie looked at it, and saw that the big gilt owl which was on the top of it had drooped its wings so that they covered the whole of the clock, and had stretched its cat-like head, with the crooked beak, a long way forward. And the 'warning' kept growing louder and louder, with distinct words: 'Clocks, clockies, stop ticking. No sound, but cautious "warning." Mousey king's ears are fine. Prr-prr. Only sing "poom, poom"; sing the olden song of doom! prr-prr; poom, poom. Bells go chime! Soon rings out the fated time!' And then came 'Poom! poom!' quite hoarsely and smothered, twelve times.

"Marie grew terribly frightened, and was going to rush away as best she could, when she noticed that Godpapa Drosselmeier was up on the top of the clock instead of the owl, with his yellow coat-tails hanging down on both sides, like wings. But she manned herself, and called out in a loud voice of anguish:

"Godpapa! godpapa! what are you up there for? Come down to me, and don't frighten me so terribly, you naughty, naughty Godpapa Drosselmeier!'

"But then there begun a sort of wild kickering and queaking, everywhere, all about, and presently there was a sound as of running and trotting, as of thousands of little feet behind the walls, and thousands of little lights began to glitter out between the chinks of the woodwork. But they were not lights; no, no! little glittering eyes; and Marie became aware that, everywhere, mice were peeping and squeezing themselves out through every chink. Presently they were trotting and galloping in all directions over the room; orderly bodies, continually increasing, of mice, forming themselves into regular troops and squadrons, in good order, just as Fritz's soldiers did when manœuvres were going on. As Marie was not afraid of mice (as many children are), she could not help being amused by this, and her first alarm had nearly left her, when suddenly there came such a sharp and terrible piping noise that the blood ran cold in her veins. Ah! what did she see then? Well, truly, kind reader, I know that your heart is in the right place, just as much as my friend Field Marshal Fritz's is, itself, but if you had seen what now came before Marie's eyes, you would have made a clean pair of heels of it; nay, I consider that you would have plumped into your bed, and drawn the blankets further over your head than necessity demanded.

"But poor Marie hadn't it in her power to do any such thing, because, right at her feet, as if impelled by some

subterranean power, sand, and lime, and broken stone came
bursting up, and then seven mouse-heads, with seven shining
crowns upon them, rose through the floor, hissing and piping
in a most horrible way. Quickly the body of the mouse which
had those seven crowned heads forced its way up through
the floor, and this enormous creature shouted, with its seven
heads, aloud to the assembled multitude, squeaking to them
with all the seven mouths in full chorus; and then the entire
army set itself in motion, and went trot, trot, right up to the
cupboard--and, in fact, to Marie, who was standing beside it.

"Marie's heart had been beating so with terror that she
had thought it must jump out of her breast, and she must die.
But now it seemed to her as if the blood in her veins stood
still. Half fainting, she leant backwards, and then there was
a 'klirr, klirr, prr,' and the pane of the cupboard, which she
had broken with her elbow, fell in shivers to the floor. She
felt, for a moment, a sharp, stinging pain in her arm, but still,
this seemed to make her heart lighter; she heard no more of
the queaking and piping. Everything was quiet; and though
she didn't dare to look, she thought the noise of the glass
breaking had frightened the mice back to their holes.

"But what came to pass then? Right behind Marie a
movement seemed to commence in the cupboard, and small,
faint voices began to be heard, saying:

'Come, awake, measures take;
Out to the fight, out to the fight;
Shield the right, shield the right;

27

Aim and away, this is the night.'

And harmonica-bells began ringing as prettily as you please.

"Oh! that's my little peal of bells!' cried Marie, and went nearer and looked in. Then she saw that there was bright light in the cupboard, and everything busily in motion there; dolls and little figures of various kinds all running about together, and struggling with their little arms. At this point, Nutcracker rose from his bed, cast off the bedclothes, and sprung with both feet on to the floor (of the shelf), crying out at the top of his voice:

'Knack, knack, knack,
Stupid mousey pack,
All their skulls we'll crack.
Mousey pack, knack, knack,
Mousey pack, crick and crack,
Cowardly lot of schnack!'

"And with this he drew his little sword, waved it in the air, and cried:
Ye, my trusty vassals, brethren and friends, are ye ready to stand by me in this great battle?'

"Immediately three scaramouches, one pantaloon, four chimney-sweeps, two zither-players, and a drummer cried, in eager accents:
Yes, your highness; we will stand by you in loyal duty; we

will follow you to the death, the victory, and the fray!' And they precipitated themselves after Nutcracker (who, in the excitement of the moment, had dared that perilous leap) to the bottom shelf. Now they might well dare this perilous leap, for not only had they got plenty of clothes on, of cloth and silk, but besides, there was not much in their insides except cotton and sawdust, so that they plumped down like little wool-sacks. But as for poor Nutcracker, he would certainly have broken his anus and legs; for, bethink you, it was nearly two feet from where he had stood to the shelf below, and his body was as fragile as if he had been made of elm-wood. Yes, Nutcracker would have broken his arms and legs, had not Miss Clara started up, at the moment of his spring, from her sofa, and received the hero, drawn sword and all, in her tender arms.

Oh! you dear, good Clara!' cried Marie, 'how I did misunderstand you. I believe you were quite willing to let dear Nutcracker have your bed.'

"But Miss Clara now cried, as she pressed the young hero gently to her silken breast:

Oh, my lord! go not into this battle and danger, sick and wounded as you are. See how your trusty vassals, clowns and pantaloon, chimney-sweeps, zithermen and drummer, are already arrayed below; and the puzzle-figures, in my shelf here, are in motion, and preparing for the fray! Deign, then, oh my lord, to rest in these arms of mine, and contemplate your victory from a safe coign of vantage.'

"Thus spoke Clara. But Nutcracker behaved so impatiently,

and kicked so with his legs, that Clara was obliged to put him down on the shelf in a hurry. However, he at once sank gracefully on one knee, and expressed himself as follows:

Oh, lady! the kind protection and aid which you have afforded me, will ever be present to my heart, in battle and in victory!'

"On this, Clara bowed herself so as to be able to take hold of him by his arms, raised him gently up, quickly loosed her girdle, which was ornamented with many spangles, and would have placed it about his shoulders. But the little man drew himself swiftly two steps back, laid his hand upon his heart, and said, with much solemnity:

"Oh, lady! do not bestow this mark of your favour upon me; for----' He hesitated, gave a deep sigh, took the ribbon, with which Marie had bound him, from his shoulders, pressed it to his lips, put it on as a cognizance for the fight, and, waving his glittering sword, sprang, like a bird, over the ledge of the cupboard down to the floor.

"You will observe, kind reader, that Nutcracker, even before he really came to life, had felt and understood all Marie's goodness and regard, and that it was because of his gratitude and devotion to her, that he would not take, or wear even, a ribbon of Miss Clara's, although it was exceedingly pretty and charming. This good, true-hearted Nutcracker preferred Marie's much commoner and more unpretending token.

"But what is going to happen, further, now? At the moment when Nutcracker sprang down, the queaking and piping commenced again worse than ever. Alas! under the big table, the hordes of the mouse army had taken up a position, densely massed, under the command of the terrible mouse with the seven heads. So what is to be the result?

THE BATTLE.

"Beat the Generale, trusty vassal-drummer!' cried Nutcracker, very loud; and immediately the drummer began to roll his drum in the most splendid style, so that the windows of the glass cupboard rattled and resounded. Then there began a cracking and a clattering inside, and Marie saw all the lids of the boxes in which Fritz's army was quartered bursting open, and the soldiers all came out and jumped down to the bottom shelf, where they formed up in good order. Nutcracker hurried up and down the ranks, speaking words of encouragement.

There's not a dog of a trumpeter taking the trouble to sound a call!' he cried in a fury. Then he turned to the pantaloon (who was looking decidedly pale), and, wobbling his long chin a good deal, said, in a tone of solemnity:

I know how brave and experienced you are, General! What is essential here, is a rapid comprehension of the situation, and immediate utilization of the passing moment. I entrust you with the command of the cavalry and artillery. You can do without a horse; your own legs are long, and you can gallop on them as fast as is necessary. Do your duty!'

"Immediately Pantaloon put his long, lean fingers to his month, and gave such a piercing crow that it rang as if a hundred little trumpets had been sounding lustily. Then there began a tramping and a neighing in the cupboard; and Fritz's dragoons and cuirassiers--but above all, the new glittering hussars--marched out, and thru came to a halt, drawn up on the floor. They then marched past Nutcracker by regiments, with guidons flying and bands playing; after which they wheeled into line, and formed up at right angles to the line of march. Upon this, Fritz's artillery came rattling up, and formed action front in advance of the halted cavalry. Then it went 'boom-boom!' and Marie saw the sugar-plums doing terrible execution amongst the thickly-massed mouse-battalions, which were powdered quite white by them, and greatly put to shame. But a battery of heavy guns, which had taken up a strong position on mamma's footstool, was what did the greatest execution; and 'poom-poom-poom!' kept up a murderous fire of gingerbread nuts into the enemy's ranks with most destructive effect, mowing the mice down in great numbers. The enemy, however, was not materially checked in his advance, and had even possessed himself of one or two of the heavy guns, when there came 'prr-prr-prr!' and Marie could scarcely see what was happening, for smoke and dust; but this much is certain, that every corps engaged fought with the utmost bravery and determination, and it was for a long time doubtful which side would gain the day. The mice kept on developing fresh bodies of their forces, as they were advanced to the scene of action; their little silver balls--like pills in size--which they delivered with great precision (their musketry practice being specially fine) took effect even inside the glass cupboard. Clara and Gertrude ran up and down in utter despair, wringing their hands, and loudly lamenting.

"Must I--the very loveliest doll in all the world--perish miserably in the very flower of my youth?' cried Miss Clara.

Oh! was it for this,' wept Gertrude, 'that I have taken such pains to conserver myself all these years? Must I be shot here in my own drawing-room after all?"

"On this, they fell into each other's arms, and howled so terribly that you could hear them above all the din of the battle. For you have no idea of the hurly-burly that went on now, dear auditor! It went prr-prr-poof, piff-schnetterdeng--schnetterdeng--boom-booroom--boom-booroom--boom all confusedly and higgledy-piggledy; and the mouse-king and the mice squeaked and screamed; and then again Nutcracker's powerful voice was heard shouting words of command, and issuing important orders, and he was seen striding along amongst his battalions in the thick of the fire.

'Pantaloon had made several most brilliant cavalry charges, and covered himself with glory. But Fritz's hussars were subjected--by the mice--to a heavy fire of very evil-smelling shot, which made horrid spots on their red tunics; this caused them to hesitate, and hang rather back for a time. Pantaloon made them take ground to the left, in échelon, and, in the excitement of the moment, he, with his dragoons and cuirassiers, executed a somewhat analogous movement. That is to say, they brought up the right shoulder, wheeled to the left, and marched home to their quarters. This had the effect of bringing the battery of artillery on the footstool into imminent danger, and it was not long before a large body of exceedingly ugly mice delivered such a vigorous assault on this position that the whole of the footstool, with the guns and gunners, fell into the enemy's hands. Nutcracker seemed much disconcerted, and ordered his right wing to commence a retrograde movement. A soldier of your experience, my dear Fritz, knows well that such a movement is almost tantamount to a regular retreat, and you grieve, with me, in anticipation, for the disaster which threatens the army of Marie's beloved little Nutcracker. But turn your glance in the other direction, and look at this left wing of Nutcracker's, where all is still going well, and you will see that there is yet much hope for the commander-in-chief and his cause.

"During the hottest part of the engagement masses of mouse-cavalry had been quietly debouching from under the chest of drawers, and had subsequently made a most determined advance upon the left wing of Nutcracker's force, uttering loud and horrible queakings. But what a reception they met with! Very slowly, as the nature the terrain necessitated (for the ledge at the bottom of the cupboard had to be passed), the regiment of motto-figures, commanded by two Chinese Emperors, advanced, and formed square. These fine, brilliantly-uniformed troops, consisting of gardeners, Tyrolese, Tungooses, hairdressers, harlequins, Cupids, lions, tigers, unicorns, and monkeys, fought with the utmost courage, coolness, and steady endurance. This bataillon d'élite would have wrested the victory from the enemy had not one of his cavalry captains, pushing forward in a rash and foolhardy manner, made a charge upon one of the Chinese Emperors, and bitten off his head. This Chinese Emperor, in his fall, knocked over and smothered a couple of Tungooses and a unicorn, and this created a gap, through which the enemy effected a rush, which resulted in the whole battalion being bitten to death. But the enemy gained little advantage by this; for as soon as one of the mouse-cavalry soldiers bit one of these brave adversaries to death, he found that there was a small piece of printed paper sticking in his throat, of which he died in a moment. Still, this was of small advantage to Nutcracker's army, which, having once commenced a retrograde movement, went on retreating farther and farther, suffering greater and greater loss. So that the unfortunate Nutcracker found himself driven back close to the front of the cupboard, with a very small remnant of his army.

Bring up the reserves! Pantaloon! Scaramouch! Drummer! where the devil have you got to?' shouted Nutcracker, who was still reckoning on reinforcements from the cupboard. And there did, in fact, advance a small contingent of brown gingerbread men and women, with gilt faces, hats, and helmets; but they laid about them so clumsily that they never hit any of the enemy, and soon knocked off the cap of their commander-in-chief, Nutcracker, himself. And the enemy's chasseurs soon bit their legs off, so that they tumbled topsy-turvy, and killed several of Nutcracker's companions-in-arms into the bargain.

"Nutcracker was now hard pressed, and closely hemmed in by the enemy, and in a position of extreme peril, He tried to jump the bottom ledge of the cupboard, but his legs were not long enough. Clara and Gertrude had fainted; so they could give him no assistance. Hussars and heavy dragoons came charging up at him, and he shouted in wild despair:

A horse! a horse! My kingdom for a horse!'

"At this moment two of the enemy's riflemen seized him by his wooden cloak, and the king of the mice went rushing up to him, squeaking in triumph out of all his seven throats.

"Marie could contain herself no longer. 'Oh! my poor Nutcracker!' she sobbed, took her left shoe off, without very distinctly knowing what she was about, and threw it as hard as she could into the thick of the enemy, straight at their king.

"Instantly everything vanished and disappeared. All was silence. Nothing to be seen. But Marie felt a more stinging pain than before in her left arm, and fell on the floor insensible.

THE INVALID.

"When Marie awoke from a death-like sleep she was lying in her little bed; and the sun was shining brightly in at the window, which was all covered with frost-flowers. There was a stranger gentleman sitting beside her, whom she recognized as Dr. Wendelstern. 'She's awake,' he said softly, and her mother came and looked at her very scrutinizingly and anxiously.

Oh, mother!' whispered Marie, 'are all those horrid mice gone away, and is Nutcracker quite safe?'

Don't talk such nonsense, Marie,' answered her mother. 'What have the mice to do with Nutcracker? You're a very naughty girl, and have caused us all a great deal of anxiety. See what comes of children not doing as they're told! You were playing with your toys so late last night that you fell asleep. I don't know whether or not some mouse jumped out and frightened you, though there are no mice here, generally. But, at all events, you broke a pane of the glass cupboard with your elbow, and cut your arm so bally that Dr. Wendelstern (who has just taken a number of pieces of the glass out of your arm) thinks that if it had been only a little higher up you might have had a stiff arm for life, or even have bled to death. Thank Heaven, I awoke about twelve o'clock and missed you; and I found you lying insensible in front of the glass cupboard, bleeding frightfully, with a number of Fritz's lead soldiers scattered round you, and other toys, broken motto-figures, and gingerbread men; and Nutcracker was lying on your bleeding arm, with your left shoe not far off.'

"Oh, mother, mother,' said Marie, 'these were the remains of the tremendous battle between the toys and the mice; and what frightened me so terribly was that the mice were going to take Nutcracker (who was the commander-in-chief of the toy army) a prisoner. Then I threw my shoe in among the mice, and after that I know nothing more that happened.'

"Dr. Wendelstern gave a significant look at the mother, who said very gently to Marie:

Never mind, dear, keep yourself quiet. The mice are all gone away, and Nutcracker's in the cupboard, quite safe and sound.'

"Here Marie's father came in, and had a long consultation with Dr. Wendelstern. Then he felt Marie's pulse, and she heard them talking about 'wound-fever.' She had to stay in bed, and take medicine, for some days, although she didn't feel at all ill, except that her arm was rather stiff and painful. She knew Nutcracker had got safe out of the battle, and she seemed to remember, as if in a dream, that he had said, quite distinctly, in a very melancholy tone:

Marie! dearest lady! I am most deeply indebted to you. But it is in your power to do even more for me still.'

"She thought and thought what this could possibly be; but in vain; she couldn't make it out. She wasn't able to play on account of her arm; and when she tried to read, or look through the picture-books, everything wavered before her eyes so strangely that she was obliged to stop. So that the days seemed very long to her, and she could scarcely pass the time till evening, when her mother came and sat at her bedside, telling and reading her all sorts of nice stories. She had just finished telling her the story of Prince Fakardin, when the door opened and in came Godpapa Drosselmeier, saying:

I've come to see with my own eyes how Marie's getting on.'

"When Marie saw Godpapa Drosselmeier in his little yellow coat, the scene of the night when Nutcracker lost the battle with the mice came so vividly back to her that she couldn't help crying out:

Oh! Godpapa Drosselmeier, how nasty you were! I saw you quite well when you were sitting on the clock, covering it all over with your wings, to prevent it from striking and frightening the mice. I heard you quite well when you called the mouse-king. Why didn't you help Nutcracker? Why didn't you help me, you nasty godpapa? It's nobody's fault but yours that I'm lying here with a bad arm.'

"Her mother, in much alarm, asked what she meant. But Drosselmeier began making extraordinary faces, and said, in a snarling voice, like a sort of chant in monotone:

Pendulums could only rattle--couldn't tick, ne'er a click; all the clockies stopped their ticking: no more clicking; then they all struck loud "cling-clang." Dollies! Don't your heads downhang! Hink and hank, and honk and hank. Doll-girls! don't your heads downhang! Cling and ring! The battle's over--Nutcracker all safe in clover. Comes the owl, on downy wing--Scares away the mouses' king. Pak and pik and pik and pook--clocks, bim-boom--grr-grr. Pendulums must click again. Tick and tack, grr and brr, prr and purr.'

"Marie fixed wide eyes of terror upon Godpapa Drosselmeier, because he was looking quite different, and far more horrid, than usual, and was jerking his right arm backwards and forwards as if he were some puppet moved by a handle. She was beginning to grow terribly frightened at him when her mother came in, and Fritz (who had arrived in the meantime) laughed heartily, crying, 'Why, godpapa, you are going on funnily! You're just like my old Jumping Jack that I threw away last month.'

"But the mother looked very grave, and said, 'This is a most extraordinary way of going on, Mr. Drosselmeier. What can you mean by it?'

My goodness!' said Drosselmeier, laughing, 'did you never hear my nice Watchmaker's Song? I always sing it to little invalids like Marie.' Then he hastened to sit down beside Marie's bed, and said to her, 'Don't be vexed with me because I didn't gouge out all the mouse-king's fourteen eyes. That couldn't be managed exactly; but, to make up for it, here's something which I know will please you greatly.'

"He dived into one of his pockets, and what he slowly, slowly brought out of it was--Nutcracker! whose teeth he had put in again quite firmly, and set his broken jaw completely to rights. Marie shouted for joy, and her mother laughed and said, 'Now you see for yourself how nice Godpapa Drosselmeier is to Nutcracker.'

But you must admit, Marie,' said her godpapa, 'that

Nutcracker is far from being what you might call a handsome fellow, and you can't say he has a pretty face. If you like I'll tell you how it was that the ugliness came into his family, and has been handed down in it from one generation to another. Did ever you hear about the Princess Pirlipat, the witch Mouseyrinks, and the clever Clockmaker?'

"I say, Godpapa Drosselmeier,' interrupted Fritz at this juncture, 'you've put Nutcracker's teeth in again all right, and his jaw isn't wobbly as it was; but what's become of his sword? Why haven't you given him a sword?'

"Oh,' cried Drosselmeier, annoyed, 'you must always be bothering and finding fault with something or other, boy. What have I to do with Nutcracker's sword? I've put his mouth to rights for him; he must look out for a sword for himself.'

"Yes, yes,' said Fritz, 'so he must, of course, if he's a right sort of fellow.'

So tell me, Marie,' continued Drosselmeier, 'if you know the story of Princess Pirlipat?'

Oh no,' said Marie. 'Tell it me, please--do tell it me!'

I hope it won't be as strange and terrible as your stories generally are,' said her mother.

Oh no, nothing of the kind,' said Drosselmeier. 'On the contrary, it's quite a funny story which I'm going to have the honour of telling this time.'

Go on then--do tell it to us,' cried the children; and Drosselmeier commenced as follows:--

THE STORY OF THE HARD NUT.

"Pirlipat's mother was a king's wife, so that, of course, she was a queen; and Pirlipat herself was a princess by birth as soon as ever she was born. The king was quite beside himself with joy over his beautiful little daughter as she lay in her cradle, and he danced round and round upon one leg, crying again and again,

"Hurrah! hurrah! hip, hip, hurrah! Did anybody ever see anything so lovely as my little Pirlipat?"

And all the ministers of state, and the generals, the presidents, and the officers of the staff, danced about on one leg, as the king did, and cried as loud as they could, "No, no- -never!"

"Indeed, there was no denying that a lovelier baby than Princess Pirlipat was never born since the world began. Her little face looked as if it were woven of the most delicate white and rose-coloured silk; her eyes were of sparkling azure, and her hair all in little curls like threads of gold. Moreover, she had come into the world with two rows of little pearly teeth, with which, two hours after her birth, she bit the Lord High Chancellor in the fingers, when he was making a careful examination of her features, so that he cried, "Oh! Gemini!" quite loud.

There are persons who assert that "Oh Lord" was the expression he employed, and opinions are still considerably divided on this point. At all events, she bit him in the fingers; and the realm learned, with much gratification, that both intelligence and discrimination dwelt within her angelical little frame.

All was joy and gladness, as I have said, save that the queen was very anxious and uneasy, nobody could tell why. One remarkable circumstance was, that she had Pirlipat's cradle most scrupulously guarded. Not only were there lifeguardsmen always at the doors of the nursery, but--over and above the two head nurses close to the cradle--there had always to be six other nurses all round the room at night. And what seemed rather a funny thing, which nobody could understand, was that each of these six nurses had always to have a cat in her lap, and to keep on stroking it all night long, so that it might never stop purring.

It is impossible that you, my reader, should know the reason of all these precautions; but I do, and shall proceed to tell you at once.

Once upon a time, many great kings and very grand princes were assembled at Pirlipat's father's court, and very great doings were toward. Tournaments, theatricals, and state balls were going on on the grandest scale, and the king, to show that he had no lack of gold and silver, made up his mind to make a good hole in the crown revenues for once, and launch out regardless of expense. Wherefore (having previously ascertained, privately, from the state head master cook that the court astronomer had indicated a propitious hour for pork-butching), he resolved to give a grand pudding-and-sausage banquet. He jumped into a state carriage, and personally invited all the kings and the princes--to a basin of soup, merely--that he might enjoy their astonishment at the magnificence of the entertainment. Then he said to the queen, very graciously:

"My darling, you know exactly how I like my puddings and sausages!"

"The queen quite understood what this meant. It meant that she should undertake the important duty of making the puddings and the sausages herself, which was a thing she had done on one or two previous occasions. So the chancellor of the exchequer was ordered to issue out of store the great golden sausage-kettle, and the silver casseroles. A great fire of sandal-wood was kindled, the queen put on her damask kitchen apron, and soon the most delicious aroma of pudding-broth rose steaming out of the kettle. This sweet smell penetrated into the very council chamber. The king could not control himself.

"Excuse me for a few minutes, my lords and gentlemen," he cried, rushed to the kitchen, embraced the queen, stirred in the kettle a little with his golden sceptre, and then went back, easier in his mind, to the council chamber.

The important juncture had now arrived when the fat had to be cut up into little square pieces, and browned on silver spits. The ladies-in-waiting retired, because the queen, from motives of love and duty to her royal consort, thought it proper to perform this important task in solitude. But when the fat began to brown, a delicate little whispering voice made itself audible, saying, "Give me some of that, sister! I want some of it, too; I am a queen as well as yourself; give me some."

The queen knew well who was speaking. It was Dame Mouseyrinks, who had been established in the palace for many years. She claimed relationship to the royal family, and she was queen of the realm of Mousolia herself, and lived with a considerable retinue of her own under the kitchen hearth. The queen was a kind-hearted, benevolent woman; and, although she didn't exactly care to recognize Dame Mouseyrinks as a sister and a queen, she was willing, at this festive season, to spare her the tit-bits she had a mind to. So she said, "Come out, then, Dame Mouseyrinks; of course you shall taste my browned fat."

So Dame Mouseyrinks came running out as fast as she could, held up her pretty little paws, and took morsel after morsel of the browned fat as the queen held them out to her. But then all Dame Mouseyrink's uncles, and her cousins, and her aunts, came jumping out too; and her seven sons (who were terrible ne'er-do-weels) into the bargain; and they all set-to at the browned fat, and the queen was too frightened to keep them at bay. Most fortunately the mistress of the robes came in, and drove these importunate visitors away, so that a little of the browned fat was left; and this, when the court mathematician (an ex-senior wrangler of his university) was called in (which he had to be, on purpose), it was found possible, by means of skilfully devised apparatus provided with special micrometer screws, and so forth, to apportion and distribute amongst the whole of the sausages, &c., under construction.

The kettledrums and the trumpets summoned all the great princes and potentates to the feast. They assembled in their robes of state; some of them on white palfreys, some in crystal coaches. The king received them with much gracious ceremony, and took his seat at the head of the table, with his crown on, and his sceptre in his hand. Even during the serving of the white pudding course, it was observed that he turned pale, and raised his eyes to heaven; sighs heaved his bosom; some terrible inward pain was clearly raging within him. But when the black-puddings were handed round, he fell back in his seat, loudly sobbing and groaning.

Every one rose from the table, and the court physician tried in vain to feel his pulse. Ultimately, after the administration of most powerful remedies--burnt feathers, and the like-- his majesty seemed to recover his senses to some extent, and stammered, scarce audibly, the words: "Too little fat!"

The queen cast herself down at his feet in despair, and cried, in a voice broken by sobs, "Oh, my poor unfortunate royal consort! Ah, what tortures you are doomed to endure! But see the culprit here at your feet! Punish her severely! Alas! Dame Mouseyrinks, her uncles, her seven sons, her cousins and her aunts, came and ate up nearly all the fat-- and----

"Here the queen fell back insensible.

But the king jumped up, all anger, and cried in a terrible voice, "Mistress of the robes, what is the meaning of this?"

"The mistress of the robes told all she knew, and the king resolved to take revenge on Dame Mouseyrinks and her family for eating up the fat which ought to have been in the sausages. The privy council was summoned, and it was resolved that Dame Mouseyrinks should be tried for her life, and all her property confiscated. But as his majesty was of opinion that she might go on consuming the fat, which was his appanage, the whole matter was referred to the court Clockmaker and Arcanist--whose name was the same as mine--Christian Elias Drosselmeier, and he undertook to expel Dame Mouseyrinks and all her relations from the palace precincts forever, by means of a certain politico-diplomatic procedure. He invented certain ingenious little machines, into which pieces of browned fat were inserted; and he placed these machines down all about the dwelling of Dame Mouseyrinks. Now she herself was much too knowing not to see through Drosselmeier's artifice; but all her remonstrances and warnings to her relations were unavailing. Enticed by the fragrant odour of the browned fat, all her seven sons, and a great many of her uncles, her cousins and her aunts, walked into Drosselmeier's little machines, and were immediately taken prisoners by the fall of a small grating; after which they met with a shameful death in the kitchen.

"Dame Mouseyrinks left this scene of horror with her small following. Rage and despair filled her breast. The court rejoiced greatly; the queen was very anxious, because she knew Dame Mouseyrinks' character, and knew well that she would never allow the death of her sons and other relatives to go unavenged. And, in fact, one day when the queen was cooking a fricassée of sheep's lights for the king (a dish to which he was exceedingly partial), Dame Mouseyrinks suddenly made her appearance, and said: "My sons and my uncles, my cousins and my aunts, are now no more. Have a care, lady, lest the queen of the mice bites your little princess in two! Have a care!"

"With which she vanished, and was no more seen. But the queen was so frightened that she dropped the fricassée into the fire; so this was the second time Dame Mouseyrinks spoiled one of the king's favourite dishes, at which he was very irate.

But this is enough for to-night; we'll go on with the rest of it another time.'

"Sorely as Marie--who had ideas of her own about this story--begged Godpapa Drosselmeier to go on with it, he would not be persuaded, but jumped up, saying, 'Too much at a time wouldn't be good for you; the rest to-morrow.'

"Just as Drosselmeier was going out of the door, Fritz said: I say, Godpapa Drosselmeier, was it really you who invented mousetraps?'

How can you ask such silly questions?' cried his mother. But Drosselmeier laughed oddly, and said: 'Well, you know I'm a clever clockmaker. Mousetraps had to be invented some time or other.'

"And now you know, children,' said Godpapa Drosselmeier the next evening, 'why it was the queen took such precautions about her little Pirlipat. Had she not always the fear before her eyes of Dame Mouseyrinks coming back and carrying out her threat of biting the princess to death?

Drosselmeier's ingenious machines were of no avail against the clever, crafty Dame Mouseyrinks, and nobody save the court astronomer, who was also state astrologer and reader of the stars, knew that the family of the Cat Purr had the power to keep her at bay. This was the reason why each of the lady nurses was obliged to keep one of the sons of that family (each of whom was given the honorary rank and title of "privy councillor of legation") in her lap, and render his onerous duty less irksome by gently scratching his back.

"One night, just after midnight, one of the chief nurses stationed close to the cradle, woke suddenly from a profound sleep. Everything lay buried in slumber. Not a purr to be heard--deep, deathlike silence, so that the death-watch ticking in the wainscot sounded quite loud. What were the feelings of this principal nurse when she saw, close beside her, a great, hideous mouse, standing on its hind legs, with its horrid head laid on the princess's face! She sprang up with a scream of terror. Everybody awoke; but then Dame Mouseyrinks (for she was the great big mouse in Pirlipat's cradle) ran quickly away into the corner of the room. The privy councillors of legation dashed after her, but too late! She was off and away through a chink in the floor. The noise awoke Pirlipat, who cried terribly. "Heaven be thanked, she is still alive!" cried all the nurses; but what was their horror when they looked at Pirlipat, and saw what the beautiful, delicate little thing had turned into. An enormous bloated head (instead of the pretty little golden-haired one), at the top of a diminutive, crumpled-up body, and green, wooden-looking eyes staring, where the lovely azure-blue pair had been, whilst her mouth had stretched across from the one ear to the other.

Of course the queen nearly died of weeping and loud lamentation, and the walls of the king's study had all to be hung with padded arras, because he kept on banging his head against them, crying:

"Oh! wretched king that I am! Oh, wretched king that I am!"

Of course he might have seen, then, that it would have been much better to eat his puddings with no fat in them at all, and let Dame Mouseyrinks and her folk stay on under the hearthstone. But Pirlipat's royal father thought not of that. What he did was to lay all the blame on the court Clockmaker and Arcanist, Christian Elias Drosselmeier, of Nürnberg. Wherefore he promulgated a sapient edict to the effect that said Drosselmeier should, within the space of four weeks, restore Princess Pirlipat to her pristine condition,--or, at least, indicate an unmistakable and reliable process whereby that might be accomplished,--or else suffer a shameful death by the axe of the common headsman.

Drosselmeier was not a little alarmed; but he soon began to place confidence in his art, and in his luck; so he proceeded to execute the first operation which seemed to him to be expedient. He took Princess Pirlipat very carefully to pieces, screwed off her hands and her feet, and examined her interior structure. Unfortunately, he found that the bigger she got the more deformed she would be, so that he didn't see what was to be done at all. He put her carefully together again, and sank down beside her cradle--which he wasn't allowed to go away from--in the deepest dejection.

The fourth week had come, and Wednesday of the fourth week, when the king came in, with eyes gleaming with anger, made threatening gestures with his sceptre, and cried:

"Christian Elias Drosselmeier, restore the princess, or prepare for death!"

Drosselmeier began to weep bitterly. The little princess kept on cracking nuts, an occupation which seemed to afford her much quiet satisfaction. For the first time the Arcanist was struck by Pirlipat's remarkable appetite for nuts, and the circumstance that she had been born with teeth. And the fact had been that immediately after her transformation she had begun to cry, and she had gone on crying till by chance she got hold of a nut. She at once cracked it, and ate the kernel, after which she was quite quiet. From that time her nurses found that nothing would do but to go on giving her nuts.

"Oh, holy instinct of nature--eternal, mysterious, inscrutable Interdependence of Things!" cried Drosselmeier, "thou pointest out to me the door of the secret. I will knock, and it shall be opened unto me."

He at once begged for an interview with the Court Astronomer, and was conducted to him closely guarded. They embraced, with many tears, for they were great friends, and then retired into a private closet, where they referred to many books treating of sympathies, antipathies, and other mysterious subjects. Night came on. The Court Astronomer consulted the stars, and, with the assistance of Drosselmeier (himself an adept in astrology), drew the princess's horoscope. This was an exceedingly difficult operation, for the lines kept getting more and more entangled and confused for ever so long. But at last--oh what joy!--it lay plain before them that all the princess had to do to be delivered from the enchantment which made her so hideous, and get back her former beauty, was to eat the sweet kernel of the nut Crackatook.

Now this nut Crackatook had a shell so hard that you might have fired a forty-eight pounder at it without producing the slightest effect on it. Moreover, it was essential that this nut should be cracked, in the princess's presence, by the teeth of a man whose beard had never known a razor, and who had never had on boots. This man had to hand the kernel to her with his eyes closed, and he might not open them till he had made seven steps backwards without a stumble.

Drosselmeier and the astronomer had been at work on this problem uninterruptedly for three days and three nights; and on the Saturday the king was sitting at dinner, when Drosselmeier--who was to have been beheaded on the Sunday morning--burst joyfully in to announce that he had found out what had to be done to restore Princess Pirlipat to her pristine beauty. The king embraced him in a burst of rapture, and promised him a diamond sword, four decorations, and two Sunday suits.

"Set to work immediately after dinner," the monarch cried: adding, kindly, "Take care, dear Arcanist, that the young unshaven gentleman in shoes, with the nut Crackatook all ready in his hand, is on the spot; and be sure that he touches no liquor beforehand, so that he mayn't trip up when he makes his seven backward steps like a crab. He can get as drunk as a lord afterwards, if he likes."

Drosselmeier was dismayed at this utterance of the king's, and stammered out, not without trembling and hesitation, that, though the remedy was discovered, both the nut Crackatook and the young gentleman who was to crack it had still to be searched for, and that it was matter of doubt whether they ever would be got hold of at all. The king, greatly incensed, whirled his sceptre round his crowned head, and shouted, in the voice of a lion:

"Very well, then you must be beheaded!"

It was exceedingly fortunate for the wretched Drosselmeier that the king had thoroughly enjoyed his dinner that day, and was consequently in an admirable temper, and disposed to listen to the sensible advice which the queen, who was very sorry for Drosselmeier, did not spare to give him. Drosselmeier took heart, and represented that he really had fulfilled the conditions, and discovered the necessary measures, and had gained his life, consequently. The king said this was all bosh and nonsense; but at length, after two or three glasses of liqueurs, decreed that Drosselmeier and the astronomer should start off immediately, and not come back without the nut Crackatook in their pockets. The man who was to crack it (by the queen's suggestion) might be heard of by means of advertisements in the local and foreign newspapers and gazettes.'

"Godpapa Drosselmeier interrupted his story at this point, and promised to finish it on the following evening.

"Next evening, as soon as the lights were brought, Godpapa Drosselmeier duly arrived, and went on with his story as follows:--

Drosselmeier and the court astronomer had been journeying for fifteen long years without finding the slightest trace of the nut Crackatook. I might go on for more than four weeks telling you where all they had been, and what extraordinary things they had seen. I shall not do so, however, but merely mention that Drosselmeier, in his profound discouragement, at last began to feel a most powerful longing to see his dear native town of Nürnberg once again. And he was more powerfully moved by this longing than usual one day, when he happened to be smoking a pipe of kanaster with his friend in the middle of a great forest in Asia, and he cried:

"Oh, Nürnberg, Nürnberg! dear native town--he who still knows thee not, place of renown--though far he has travelled, and great cities seen--as London, and Paris, and Peterwardeen--knoweth not what it is happy to be-- still must his longing heart languish for thee--for thee, O Nürnberg, exquisite town--where the houses have windows both upstairs and down!"

As Drosselmeier lamented thus dolefully, the astronomer, seized with compassionate sympathy, began to weep and howl so terribly that he was heard throughout the length and breadth of Asia. But he collected himself again, wiped the tears from his eyes, and said:

"After all, dearest colleague, why should we sit and weep and howl here? Why not come to Nürnberg? Does it matter a brass farthing, after all, where and how we search for this horrible nut Crackatook?"

"That's true, too," answered Drosselmeier, consoled. They both got up immediately, knocked the ashes out of their pipes, started off, and travelled straight on without stopping, from that forest right in the centre of Asia till they came to Nürnberg. As soon as they got there, Drosselmeier went straight to his cousin the toy maker and doll-carver, and gilder and varnisher, whom he had not seen for a great many long years. To him he told all the tale of Princess Pirlipat, Dame Mouseyrinks, and the nut Crackatook, so that he clapped his hands repeatedly, and cried in amazement:

"Dear me, cousin, these things are really wonderful--very wonderful, indeed!"

Drosselmeier told him, further, some of the adventures he had met with on his long journey--how he had spent two years at the court of the King of Dates; how the Prince of Almonds had expelled him with ignominy from his territory; how he had applied in vain to the Natural History Society at Squirreltown--in short, how he had been everywhere utterly unsuccessful in discovering the faintest trace of the nut Crackatook. During this narrative, Christoph Zacharias had kept frequently snapping his fingers, twisting himself round on one foot, smacking with his tongue, etc.; then he cried:

"Ee--aye--oh!--that really would be the very deuce and all."

At last he threw his hat and wig in the air, warmly embraced his cousin, and cried:

"Cousin, cousin, you're a made man--a made man you are--for either I am much deceived, or I have got the nut Crackatook myself!"

He immediately produced a little cardboard box, out of which he took a gilded nut of medium size.

"Look there!" he said, showing this nut to his cousin; "the state of matters as regards this nut is this. Several years ago, at Christmas time, a stranger man came here with a sack of nuts, which he offered for sale. Just in front of my shop he got into a quarrel, and put the sack down the better to defend himself from the nut-sellers of the place, who attacked him. Just then a heavily-loaded waggon drove over the sack, and all the nuts were smashed but one. The stranger man, with an odd smile, offered to sell me this nut for a twenty-kreuzer piece of the year 1796. This struck me as strange. I found just such a coin in my pocket, so I bought the nut, and I gilt it over, though I didn't know why I took the trouble quite, or should have given so much for it."

All question as to its being really the long-sought nut Crackatook was dispelled when the Court Astronomer carefully scraped away the gilding, and found the word "Crackatook" graven on the shell in Chinese characters.

"The joy of the exiles was great, as you may imagine; and the cousin was even happier, for Drosselmeier assured him that he was a made man too, as he was sure of a good pension, and all the gold leaf he would want for the rest of his life for his gilding, free, gratis, for nothing.

The Arcanist and the Astronomer had both got on their nightcaps, and were going to turn into bed, when the astronomer said:

"I tell you what it is, dear colleague, one piece of good fortune never comes alone. I feel convinced that we've not only found the nut, but the young gentleman who is to crack it, and hand the beauty-restoring kernel to the princess, into the bargain. I mean none other than your cousin's son here, and I don't intend to close an eye this night till I've drawn that youngster's horoscope."

With which he threw away his nightcap, and at once set to work to consult the stars. The cousin's son was a nice-looking, well-grown young fellow, had never been shaved, and had never worn boots. True, he had been a Jumping Jack for a Christmas or two in his earlier days, but there was scarcely any trace of this discoverable about him, his appearance had been so altered by his father's care. He had appeared last Christmas in a beautiful red coat with gold trimmings, a sword by his side, his hat under his arm, and a fine wig with a pigtail. Thus apparelled, he stood in his father's shop exceeding lovely to behold, and from his native galanterie he occupied himself in cracking nuts for the young ladies, who called him "the handsome nutcracker."

Next morning the Astronomer fell, with much emotion, into the Arcanist's arms, crying:

"This is the very man!--we have got him!--he is found! Only, dearest colleague, two things we must keep carefully in view. In the first place, we must construct a most substantial pigtail for this precious nephew of yours, which shall be connected with his lower jaw in such sort that it shall be capable of communicating a very powerful pull to it. And next, when we get back to the Residenz, we must carefully conceal the fact that we have brought the young gentleman who is to shiver the nut back with us. He must not make his appearance for a considerable time after us. I read in the horoscope that if two or three others bite at the nut unsuccessfully to begin with, the king will promise the man who breaks it,--and, as a consequence, restores the princess her good looks,--the princess's hand and the succession to the crown."

"The doll-maker cousin was immensely delighted with the idea of his son's marrying Princess Pirlipat, and being a prince and king, so he gave him wholly over to the envoys to do what they liked with him. The pigtail which Drosselmeier attached to him proved to be a very powerful and efficient instrument, as he exemplified by cracking the hardest of peach-stones with the utmost ease.

Drosselmeier and the Astronomer, having at once sent the news to the Residenz of the discovery of the nut Crackatook, the necessary advertisements were at once put in the newspapers, and, by the time that our travellers got there, several nice young gentlemen, among whom there were princes even, had arrived, having sufficient confidence in their teeth to try to disenchant the princess. The ambassadors were horrified when they saw poor Pirlipat again. The diminutive body with tiny hands and feet was not big enough to support the great shapeless head. The hideousness of the face was enhanced by a beard like white cotton, which had grown about the mouth and chin. Everything had turned out as the court astronomer had read it in the horoscope. One milksop in shoes after another bit his teeth and his jaws into agonies over the nut, without doing the princess the slightest good in the world. And then, when he was carried out on the verge of insensibility by the dentists who were in attendance on purpose, he would sigh:

"Ah dear, that was a hard nut."

Now when the king, in the anguish of his soul, had promised to him who should disenchant the princess his daughter and the kingdom, the charming, gentle young Drosselmeier made his appearance, and begged to be allowed to make an attempt. None of the previous ones had pleased the princess so much. She pressed her little hands to her heart and sighed:

"Ah, I hope it will be he who will crack the nut, and be my husband."

When he had politely saluted the king, the queen, and the Princess Pirlipat, he received the nut Crackatook from the hands of the Clerk of the Closet, put it between his teeth, made a strong effort with his head, and--crack--crack--the shell was shattered into a number of pieces. He neatly cleared the kernel from the pieces of husk which were sticking to it, and, making a leg, presented it courteously to the princess, after which he closed his eyes and began his backward steps. The princess swallowed the kernel, and--oh marvel!--the monstrosity vanished, and in its place there stood a wonderfully beautiful lady, with a face which seemed woven of delicate lily-white and rose-red silk, eyes of sparkling azure, and hair all in little curls like threads of gold.

Trumpets and kettledrums mingled in the loud rejoicings of the populace. The king and all his court danced about on one leg, as they had done at Pirlipat's birth, and the queen had to be treated with Eau de Cologne, having fallen into a fainting fit from joy and delight. All this tremendous tumult interfered not a little with young Drosselmeier's self-possession, for he still had to make his seven backward steps. But he collected himself as best he could, and was just stretching out his right foot to make his seventh step, when up came Dame Mouseyrinks through the floor, making a horrible weaking and squeaking, so that Drosselmeier, as he was putting his foot down, trod upon her, and stumbled so that he almost fell. Oh misery!--all in an instant he was transmogrified, just as the princess had been before: his body all shrivelled up, and could scarcely support the great shapeless head with enormous projecting eyes, and the wide gaping mouth. In the place where his pigtail used to be a scanty wooden cloak hung down, controlling the movements of his nether jaw.

The clockmaker and the astronomer were wild with terror and consternation, but they saw that Dame Mouseyrinks was wallowing in her gore on the floor. Her wickedness had not escaped punishment, for young Drosselmeier had squashed her so in the throat with the sharp point of his shoe that she was mortally hurt.

But as Dame Mouseyrinks lay in her death agony she queaked and cheeped in a lamentable style, and cried:

"Oh, Crackatook, thou nut so hard!--Oh, fate, which none may disregard!--Hee hee, pee pee, woe's me, I cry!--since I through that hard nut must die.--But, brave young Nutcracker, I see--you soon must follow after me.--My sweet young son, with sevenfold crown--will soon bring Master Cracker down.--His mother's death he will repay--so, Nutcracker, beware that day!--Oh, life most sweet, I feebly cry,--I leave you now, for I must die. Queak!"

With this cry died Dame Mouseyrinks, and her body was carried out by the Court Stovelighter. Meantime nobody had been troubling themselves about young Drosselmeier. But the princess reminded the king of his promise, and he at once directed that the young hero should be conducted to his presence. But when the poor wretch came forward in his transmogrified condition the princess put both her hands to her face, and cried:

"Oh please take away that horrid Nutcracker!"

So that the Lord Chamberlain seized him immediately by his little shoulders, and shied him out at the door. The king, furious at the idea of a nutcracker being brought before him as a son-in-law, laid all the blame upon the clockmaker and the astronomer, and ordered them both to be banished for ever.

The horoscope which the astronomer had drawn in Nürnberg had said nothing about this; but that didn't hinder him from taking some fresh observations. And the stars told him that young Drosselmeier would conduct himself so admirably in his new condition that he would yet be a prince and a king, in spite of his transmogrification; but also that his deformity would only disappear after the son of Dame Mouseyrinks, the seven-headed king of the mice (whom she had born after the death of her original seven sons) should perish by his hand, and a lady should fall in love with him notwithstanding his deformity.

That is the story of the hard nut, children, and now you know why people so often use the expression "that was a hard nut," and why Nutcrackers are so ugly.'

"Thus did Godpapa Drosselmeier finish his tale. Marie thought the Princess Pirlipat was a nasty ungrateful thing. Fritz, on the other hand, was of opinion that if Nutcracker had been a proper sort of fellow he would soon have settled the mouse king's hash, and got his good looks back again.

UNCLE AND NEPHEW.

"Should any of my respected readers or listeners ever have happened to be cut by glass they will know what an exceedingly nasty thing it is, and how long it takes to get well. Marie was obliged to stay in bed a whole week, because she felt so terribly giddy whenever she tried to stand up; but at last she was quite well again, and able to jump about as of old. Things in the glass cupboard looked very fine indeed--everything new and shiny, trees and flowers and houses--toys of every kind. Above all, Marie found her dear Nutcracker again, smiling at her in the second shelf, with his teeth all sound and right. As she looked at this pet of hers with much fondness, it suddenly struck her that all Godpapa Drosselmeier's story had been about Nutcracker, and his family feud with Dame Mouseyrinks and her people. And now she knew that her Nutcracker was none other than young Mr. Drosselmeier, of Nürnberg, Godpapa Drosselmeier's delightful nephew, unfortunately under the spells of Dame Mouseyrinks. For whilst the story was being told, Marie couldn't doubt for a moment that the clever clockmaker at Pirlipat's father's court was Godpapa Drosselmeier himself.

"But why didn't your uncle help you? Why didn't he help you?' Marie cried, sorrowfully, as she felt more and more clearly every moment that in the battle, which she had witnessed, the question in dispute had been no less a matter than Nutcracker's crown and kingdom. Wern't all the other toys his subjects? And wasn't it clear that the astronomer's prophecy that he was to be rightful King of Toyland had come true?'

"Whilst the clever Marie was weighing all these things in her mind, she kept expecting that Nutcracker and his vassals would give some indications of being alive, and make some movements as she looked at them. This, however, was by no means the case. Everything in the cupboard kept quite motionless and still. Marie thought this was the effect of Dame Mouseyrinks's enchantments, and those of her seven-headed son, which still were keeping up their power.

But,' she said, 'though you're not able to move, or to say the least little word to me, dear Mr. Drosselmeier, I know you understand me, and see how very well I wish you. Always reckon on my assistance when you require it. At all events, I will ask your uncle to aid you with all has great skill and talents, whenever there may be an opportunity.'

"Nutcracker still kept quiet and motionless. But Marie fancied that a gentle sigh came breathing through the glass cupboard, which made its panes ring in a wonderful, though all but imperceptible, manner--whilst something like a little bell-toned voice seemed to sing:

"Marie fine, angel mine! I will be thine, if thou wilt be mine!'

"Although a sort of cold shiver ran through her at this, still it caused her the keenest pleasure.

"Twilight came on. Marie's father came in with Godpapa Drosselmeier, and presently Louise set out the tea-table, and the family took their places round it, talking in the pleasantest and merriest manner about all sorts of things. Marie had taken her little stool, and sat down at her godpapa's feet in silence. When everybody happened to cease talking at the same time, Marie looked her godpapa full in the face with her great blue eyes, and said:

I know now, godpapa, that my Nutcracker is your nephew, young Mr. Drosselmeier from Nürnberg. The prophecy has come true: he is a king and a prince, just as your friend the astronomer said he would be. But you know as well as I do that he is at war with Dame Mouseyrinks's son--that horrid king of the mice. Why don't you help him?'

"Marie told the whole story of the battle, as she had witnessed it, and was frequently interrupted by the loud laughter of her mother and sister; but Fritz and Drosselmeier listened quite gravely.

Where in the name of goodness has the child got her head filled with all that nonsense?' cried her father.

She has such a lively imagination, you see,' said her mother; 'she dreamt it all when she was feverish with her arm.'

It is all nonsense,' cried Fritz, 'and it isn't true! my red hussars are not such cowards as all that. If they were, do you suppose I should command them?'

"But godpapa smiled strangely, and took little Marie on his knee, speaking more gently to her than ever he had been known to do before.

More is given to you, Marie dear,' he said, 'than to me, or the others. You are a born princess, like Pirlipat, and reign in a bright beautiful country. But you still have much to suffer, if you mean to befriend poor transformed Nutcracker; for the king of the mice lies in wait for him at every turn. But I cannot help him; you, and you only, can do that. So be faithful and true.'

"Neither Marie nor any of the others knew what Godpapa Drosselmeier meant by these words. But they struck Dr. Stahlbaum--the father--as being so strange that he felt Drosselmeier's pulse, and said:

There seems a good deal of congestion about the head, my dear sir. I'll just write you a little prescription.'

"But Marie's mother shook her head meditatively, and said:

I have a strong idea what Mr. Drosselmeier means, though I can't exactly put it in words.'

VICTORY.

"It was not very long before Marie was awakened one bright moonlight night by a curious noise, which came from one of the corners of her room. There was a sound as of small stones being thrown, and rolled here and there; and between whiles came a horrid cheeping and squeaking.

Oh, dear me! here come these abominable mice again!' cried Marie, in terror, and she would have awakened her mother. But the noise suddenly ceased; and she could not move a muscle--for she saw the king of the mice working himself out through a hole in the wall; and at last he came into the room, ran about in it, and got on to the little table at her bed-head with a great jump.

"Hee-hehee!' he cried; 'give me your sweetmeats! out with your cakes, marchpane and sugar-stick, gingerbread cakes! Don't pause to argue! If yield them you won't, I'll chew up Nutcracker! See if I don't!'

"As he cried out these terrible words he gnashed and chattered his teeth most frightfully, and then made off again through the hole in the wall. This frightened Marie so that she was quite pale in the morning, and so upset that she scarcely could utter a word. A hundred times she felt impelled to tell her mother or her sister, or at all events her brother, what had happened. But she thought, 'of course none of them would believe me. They would only laugh at me.'

"But she saw well enough that to succour Nutcracker she would have to sacrifice all her sweet things; so she laid out all she had of them at the bottom of the cupboard next evening.

I can't make out how the mice have got into the sitting-room,' said her mother. 'This is something quite new. There never were any there before. See, Marie, they've eaten up all your sweetmeats.'

"And so it was: the epicure mouse king hadn't found the marchpane altogether to his taste, but had gnawed all round the edges of it, so that what he had left of it had to be thrown into the ash-pit. Marie never minded about her sweetmeats, being delighted to think that she had saved Nutcracker by means of them. But what were her feelings when next night there came a queaking again close by her ear. Alas! The king of the mice was there again, with his eyes glaring worse than the night before.

"Give me your sugar toys,' he cried; give them you must, or else I'll chew Nutcracker up into dust!'

"Then he was gone again.

"Marie was very sorry. She had as beautiful a collection of sugar-toys as ever a little girl could boast of. Not only had she a charming little shepherd, with his shepherd looking after a flock of milk-white sheep, with a nice dog jumping about them, but two postmen with letters in their hands, and four couples of prettily dressed young gentlemen and most beautifully dressed young ladies, swinging in a Russian swing. Then there were two or three dancers, and behind them Farmer Feldkuemmel and the Maid of Orleans. Marie didn't much care about them; but back in the corner there was a little baby with red cheeks, and this was Marie's darling. The tears came to her eyes.

Ah!' she cried, turning to Nutcracker, 'I really will do all I can to help you. But it's very hard.'

"Nutcracker looked at her so piteously that she determined to sacrifice everything--for she remembered the mouse king with all his seven mouths wide open to swallow the poor young fellow; so that night she set down all her sugar figures in front of the cupboard, as she had the sweetmeats the night before. She kissed the shepherd, the shepherdess, and the lambs; and at last she brought her best beloved of all, the little red-cheeked baby from its corner, but did put it a little further back than the rest. Farmer Feldkuemmel and the Maid of Orleans had to stand in the front rank of all.

This is really getting too bad,' said Marie's mother the next morning; 'some nasty mouse or other must have made a hole in the glass cupboard, for poor Marie's sugar figures are all eaten and gnawed.' Marie really could not restrain her tears. But she was soon able to smile again; for she thought, 'What does it matter? Nutcracker is safe.'

"In the evening Marie's mother was telling her father and Godpapa Drosselmeier about the mischief which some mouse was doing in the children's cupboard, and her father said:

It's a regular nuisance! What a pity it is that we can't get rid of it. It's destroying all the poor child's things.'

"Fritz intervened, and remarked:

"The baker downstairs has a fine grey Councillor-of-Legation; I'll go and get hold of him, and he'll soon put a stop to it, and bite the mouse's head off, even if it's Dame Mouseyrinks herself, or her son, the king of the mice.'

Oh, yes!' said his mother, laughing, 'and jump up on to the chairs and tables, knock down the cups and glasses, and do ever so much mischief besides.'

No, no!' answered Fritz; 'the baker's Councillor-of-Legation's a very clever fellow. I wish I could walk about on the edge of the roof, as he does.'

Don't let us have a nasty cat in the house in the night-time,' said Louise, who hated cats.

"Fritz is quite right though,' said the mother; 'unless we set a trap. Haven't we got such a thing in the house?'

"Godpapa Drosselmeier's the man to get us one,' said Fritz; 'it was he who invented them, you know.' Everybody laughed. And when the mother said they did not possess such a thing, Drosselmeier said he had plenty; and he actually sent a very fine one round that day. When the cook was browning the fat, Marie--with her head full of the marvels of her godpapa's tale--called out to her:

"Ah, take care, Queen! Remember Dame Mouseyrinks and her people.' But Fritz drew his sword, and cried, 'Let them come if they dare! I'll give an account of them.' But everything about the hearth remained quiet and undisturbed. As Drosselmeier was fixing the browned fat on a fine thread, and setting the trap gently down in the glass cupboard, Fritz cried:

Now, Godpapa Clockmaker, mind that the mouse king doesn't play you some trick!'

"Ah, how did it fare with Marie that night? Something as cold as ice went tripping about on her arm, and something rough and nasty laid itself on her cheek, and cheeped and queaked in her ear. The horrible mouse king came and sat on her shoulder, foamed a blood-red foam out of all his seven mouths, and chattering and grinding his teeth, he hissed into Marie's ear:

Hiss, hiss!--keep away--don't go in there--ware of that house--don't you be caught--death to the mouse--hand out your picture-books--none of your scornful looks!--Give me your dresses--also your laces--or, if you don't, leave you I won't--Nutcracker I'll bite--drag him out of your sight--his last hour is near--so tremble for fear!--Fee, fa, fo, fum--his last hour is come!--Hee hee, pee pee--queak--queak!'

"Marie was overwhelmed with anguish and sorrow, and was looking quite pale and upset when her mother said to her next morning:

This horrid mouse hasn't been caught. But never mind, dear, we'll catch the nasty thing yet, never fear. If the traps won't do, Fritz shall fetch the grey Councillor of Legation.'

"As soon as Marie was alone, she went up to the glass cupboard, and said to Nutcracker, in a voice broken by sobs:

Ah, my dear, good Mr. Drosselmeier, what can I do for you, poor unfortunate girl that I am! Even if I give that horrid king of the mice all my picture-books, and my new dress which the Child Christ gave me at Christmas as well, he's sure to go on asking for more; so I soon shan't have anything more left, and he'll want to eat me! Oh, poor thing that I am!

What shall I do? What shall I do?'

"As she was thus crying and lamenting, she noticed that a great spot of blood had been left, since the eventful night of the battle, upon Nutcracker's neck. Since she had known that he was really young Mr. Drosselmeier, her godpapa's nephew, she had given up carrying him in her arms, and petting and kissing him; indeed, she felt a delicacy about touching him at all. But now she took him carefully out of his shelf, and began to wipe off this blood-spot with her handkerchief. What were her feelings when she found that Nutcracker was growing warmer and warmer in her hand, and beginning to move! She put him back into the cupboard as fast as she could. His mouth began to wobble backwards and forwards, and he began to whisper, with much difficulty:

Ah, dearest Miss Stahlbaum--most precious of friends! How deeply I am indebted to you for everything--for everything! But don't, don't sacrifice any of your picture-books or pretty dresses for me. Get me a sword--a sword is what I want. If you get me that, I'll manage the rest-- though--he may----'

"There Nutcracker's speech died away, and his eyes, which had been expressing the most sympathetic grief, grew staring and lifeless again.

"Marie felt no fear; she jumped for joy, rather, now that she knew how to help Nutcracker without further painful sacrifices. But where on earth was she to get hold of a sword for him? She resolved to take counsel with Fritz; and that evening, when their father and mother had gone out, and

73

they two were sitting beside the glass cupboard, she told him what had passed between her and Nutcracker with the king of the mice, and what it was that was required to rescue Nutcracker.

"The thing which chiefly exercised Fritz's mind was Marie's statement as to the unexemplary conduct of his red hussars in the great battle. He asked her once more, most seriously, to assure him if it really was the truth; and when she had repeated her statement, on her word of honour, he advanced to the cupboard, and made his hussars a most affecting address; and, as a punishment for their behaviour, he solemnly took their plumes one by one out of their busbies, and prohibited them from sounding the march of the hussars of the guard for the space of a twelvemonth. When he had performed this duty, he turned to Marie, and said:

"As far as the sword is concerned, I have it in my power to assist Nutcracker. I placed an old Colonel of Cuirassiers on retirement on a pension, no longer ago than yesterday, so that he has no further occasion for his sabre, which is sharp.'

"This Colonel was settled, on his pension, in the back corner of the third shelf. He was fetched out from thence, and his sabre--still a bright and handsome silver weapon--taken off, and girt about Nutcracker.

"Next night Marie could not close an eye for anxiety. About midnight she fancied she heard a strange stirring and noise in the sitting-room--a rustling and a clanging--and all at once came a shrill 'Queak!'

The king of the mice! The king of the mice!' she cried,

and jumped out of bed, all terror. Everything was silent; but soon there came a gentle tapping at the door of her room, and a soft voice made itself heard, saying:

"Please to open your door, dearest Miss Stahlbaum! Don't be in the least degree alarmed; good, happy news!'

"It was Drosselmeier's voice--young Drosselmeier's, I mean. She threw on her dressing-gown, and opened the door as quickly as possible. There stood Nutcracker, with his sword, all covered with blood, in his right hand, and a little wax taper in his left. When he saw Marie he knelt down on one knee, and said:

It was you, and you only, dearest lady, who inspired me with knightly valour, and steeled me with strength to do battle with the insolent caitiff who dared to insult you. The treacherous king of the mice lies vanquished and writhing in his gore! Deign, lady, to accept these tokens of victory from the hand of him who is, till death, your true and faithful knight.'

"With this Nutcracker took from his left arm the seven crowns of the mouse king, which he had ranged upon it, and handed them to Marie, who received them with the keenest pleasure. Nutcracker rose, and continued as follows:

"Oh! my best beloved Miss Stahlbaum, if you would only take the trouble to follow me for a few steps, what glorious and beautiful things I could show you, at this supreme moment when I have overcome my hereditary foe! Do--do come with me, dearest lady!'

"TOYLAND.

"I feel quite convinced, children, that none of you would have hesitated for a moment to go with good, kind Nutcracker, who had always shown himself to be such a charming person, and Marie was all the more disposed to do as he asked her, because she knew what her just claims on his gratitude were, and was sure that he would keep his word, and show her all sorts of beautiful things. So she said:

I will go with you, dear Mr. Drosselmeier; but it mustn't be very far, and it won't do to be very long, because, you know, I haven't had any sleep yet.'

Then we will go by the shortest route,' said Nutcracker, 'although it is, perhaps, rather the most difficult.'

"He went on in front, followed by Marie, till he stopped before the big old wardrobe. Marie was surprised to see that, though it was generally shut, the doors of it were now wide open, so that she could see her father's travelling cloak of fox-fur hanging in the front. Nutcracker clambered deftly up this cloak, by the edgings and trimmings of it, so as to get hold of the big tassel which was fastened at the back of it by a thick cord. He gave this tassel a tug, and a pretty little ladder of cedar-wood let itself quickly down through one of the arm-holes of the cloak.

Now, Miss Stahlbaum, step up that ladder, if you will be so kind,' said Nutcracker. Marie did so. But as soon as she had got up through the arm-hole, and begun to look out at the neck, all at once a dazzling light came streaming on to her, and she found herself standing on a lovely, sweet-scented meadow, from which millions of sparks were streaming upward, like the glitter of beautiful gems.

"This is Candy Mead, where we are now,' said Nutcracker. 'But we'll go in at that gate there.'

"Marie looked up and saw a beautiful gateway on the meadow, only a few steps off. It seemed to be made of white, brown, and raisin-coloured marble; but when she came close to it she saw it was all of baked sugar-almonds and raisins, which--as Nutcracker said when they were going through it--was the reason it was called 'Almond and Raisin Gate.' There was a gallery running round the upper part of it, apparently made of barley-sugar, and in this gallery six monkeys, dressed in red doublets, were playing on brass instruments in the most delightful manner ever heard; so that it was all that Marie could do to notice that she was walking along upon a beautiful variegated marble pavement, which, however, was really a mosaic of lozenges of all colours. Presently the sweetest of odours came breathing round her, streaming from a beautiful little wood on both sides of the way. There was such a glittering and sparkling among the dark foliage, that one could see all the gold and silver fruits hanging on the many-tinted stems, and these stems and branches were all ornamented and dressed up in ribbons and bunches of flowers, like brides and bridegrooms, and festive wedding guests. And as the orange perfume came wafted, as if on the wings of gentle zephyrs, there was a soughing among the leaves and branches, and all the goldleaf and tinsel rustled and tinkled like beautiful music, to which the sparkling lights could not help dancing.

Oh, how charming this is!' cried Marie, enraptured.

This is Christmas Wood, dearest Miss Stahlbaum,' said Nutcracker,

"Ah!' said Marie, 'if I could only stay here for a little! Oh, it is so lovely!'

"Nutcracker clapped his little hands, and immediately there appeared a number of little shepherds and shepherdesses, and hunters and huntresses, so white and delicate that you would have thought they were made of pure sugar, whom Marie had not noticed before, although they had been walking about in the wood: and they brought a beautiful gold reclining chair, laid down a white satin cushion in it, and politely invited Marie to take a seat. As soon as she did so, the shepherds and shepherdesses danced a pretty ballet, to which the hunters and huntresses played the music on their horns, and then they all disappeared amongst the thickets.

"I must really apologize for the poor style in which this dance was executed, dearest Miss Stahlbaum,' said Nutcracker. 'These people all belong to our Wire Ballet Troupe, and can only do the same thing over and over again. Had we not better go on a little farther?'

Oh, I'm sure it was all most delightful, and I enjoyed it immensely!' said Marie, as she stood up and followed Nutcracker, who was going on leading the way. They went by the side of a gently rippling brook, which seemed to be what was giving out all the perfume which filled the wood.

This is Orange Brook,' said Nutcracker; 'but, except for

its sweet scent, it is nothing like as fine a water as the River Lemonade, a beautiful broad stream, which falls--as this one does also--into the Almond-milk Sea.'

"And, indeed, Marie soon heard a louder plashing and rushing, and came in sight of the River Lemonade, which went rolling along in swelling waves of a yellowish colour, between banks covered with a herbage and underwood which shone like green carbuncles. A remarkable freshness and coolness, strengthening heart and breast, exhaled from this fine river. Not far from it a dark yellow stream crept sluggishly along, giving out a most delicious odour; and on its banks sat numbers of pretty children, angling for little fat fishes, which they ate as soon as they caught them. These fish were very much like filberts, Marie saw when she came closer. A short distance farther, on the banks of this stream, stood a nice little village. The houses of this village, and the church, the parsonage, the barns, and so forth, were all dark brown with gilt roofs, and many of the walls looked as if they were plastered over with lemon-peel and shelled almonds.

That is Gingerthorpe on the Honey River,' said Nutcracker. 'It is famed for the good looks of its inhabitants; but they are very short-tempered people, because they suffer so much from tooth-ache. So we won't go there at present.'

"At this moment Marie caught sight of a little town where the houses were all sorts of colours and quite transparent, exceedingly pretty to look at. Nutcracker went on towards this town, and Marie heard a noise of bustle and merriment, and saw some thousands of nice little folks unloading a number of waggons which were drawn up in the market-place. What they were unloading from the waggons looked like packages of coloured paper, and tablets of chocolate.

This is Bonbonville,' Nutcracker said. 'An embassy has just arrived from Paperland and the King of Chocolate. These poor Bonbonville people have been vexatiously threatened lately by the Fly-Admiral's forces, so they are covering their houses over with their presents from Paperland, and constructing fortifications with the fine pieces of workmanship which the Chocolate-King has sent them. But oh! dearest Miss Stahlbaum, we are not going to restrict ourselves to seeing the small towns and villages of this country. Let us be off to the metropolis.'

"He stepped quickly onwards, and Marie followed him, all expectation. Soon a beautiful rosy vapour began to rise, suffusing everything with a soft splendour. She saw that this was reflected from a rose-red, shining water, which went plashing and rushing away in front of them in wavelets of roseate silver. And on this delightful water, which kept broadening and broadening out wider and wider, like a great lake, the loveliest swans were floating, white as silver, with collars of gold. And, as if vieing with each other, they were singing the most beautiful songs, at which little fish, glittering like diamonds, danced up and down in the rosy ripples.

Oh!' cried Marie, in the greatest delight, 'this must be the lake which Godpapa Drosselmeier was once going to make for me, and I am the girl who is to play with the swans.'

"Nutcracker gave a sneering sort of laugh, such as she

had never seen in him before, and said:

My uncle could never make a thing of this kind. You would be much more likely to do it yourself. But don't let us bother about that. Rather let us go sailing over the water, Lake Rosa here, to the metropolis.'

THE METROPOLIS.

"Nutcracker clapped his little hands again, and the waves of Lake Rosa began to sound louder and to plash higher, and Marie became aware of a sort of car approaching from the distance, made wholly of glittering precious stones of every colour, and drawn by two dolphins with scales of gold. Twelve of the dearest little negro boys, with head-dresses and doublets made of humming-birds' feathers woven together, jumped to land, and carried first Marie and then Nutcracker, gently gliding above the water, into the car, which immediately began to move along over the lake of its own accord. Ah! how beautiful it was when Marie went onward thus over the waters in the shell-shaped car, with the rose-perfume breathing around her, and the rosy waves plashing. The two golden-scaled dolphins lifted their nostrils, and sent streams of crystal high in the air; and as these fell down in glittering, sparkling rainbows, there was a sound as of two delicate, silvery voices, singing, 'Who comes over the rosy sea?--Fairy is she. Bim-bim--fishes; sim-sim--swans; sfa-sfa--golden birds; tratrah, rosy waves, wake you, and sing, sparkle and ring, sprinkle and kling--this is the fairy we languish to see--coming at last to us over the sea. Rosy waves dash--bright dolphins play--merrily, merrily on!'

"But the twelve little black boys at the back of the car seemed to take some umbrage at this song of the water-jets; for they shook the sunshades they were holding so that the palm leaves they were made of clattered and rattled together;

82

and as they shook them they stamped an odd sort of rhythm with their feet, and sang:

Klapp and klipp, and klipp and klapp, and up and down.'

Negroes are merry, amusing fellows,' said Nutcracker, a little put out; 'but they'll set the whole lake into a state of regular mutiny on my hands!' And in fact there did begin a confused, and confusing, noise of strange voices which seemed to be floating both in the water and in the air. However, Marie paid no attention to it, but went on looking into the perfumed rosy waves, from each of which a pretty girl's face smiled back to her.

"Oh! look at Princess Pirlipat,' she cried, clapping her hands with gladness, 'smiling at me so charmingly down there! Do look at her, Mr. Drosselmeier.'

"But Nutcracker sighed, almost sorrowfully, and said:

That is not Princess Pirlipat, dearest Miss Stahlbaum, it is only yourself; always your own lovely face smiling up from the rosy waves.' At this Marie drew her head quickly back, closed her eyes as tightly as she could, and was terribly ashamed. But just then the twelve negroes lifted her out of the car and set her on shore. She found herself in a small thicket or grove, almost more beautiful even than Christmas Wood, everything glittered and sparkled so in it. And the fruit on the trees was extraordinarily wonderful and beautiful, and not only of very curious colours, but with the most delicious perfume.

Ah!' said Nutcracker, 'here we are in Comfit Grove, and yonder lies the metropolis.'

"How shall I set about describing all the wonderful and beautiful sights which Marie now saw, or give any idea of the splendour and magnificence of the city which lay stretched out before her on a flowery plain? Not only did the walls and towers of it shine in the brightest and most gorgeous colours, but the shapes and appearance of the buildings were like nothing to be seen on earth. Instead of roofs the houses had on beautiful twining crowns, and the towers were garlanded with beautiful leaf-work, sculptured and carved into exquisite, intricate designs. As they passed in at the gateway, which looked as if it was made entirely of macaroons and sugared fruits, silver soldiers presented arms, and a little man in a brocade dressing-gown threw himself upon Nutcracker's neck, crying:

Welcome, dearest prince! welcome to Sweetmeatburgh!'

"Marie wondered not a little to see such a very grand personage recognise young Mr. Drosselmeier as a prince. But she heard such a number of small delicate voices making such a loud clamouring and talking, and such a laughing and chattering going on, and such a singing and playing, that she couldn't give her attention to anything else, but asked Drosselmeier what was the meaning of it all.

Oh, it is nothing out of the common, dearest Miss Stahlbaum,' he answered. 'Sweetmeatburgh is a large, populous city, full of mirth and entertainment. This is only the usual thing that is always going on here every day. Please to come on a little farther.'

"After a few paces more they were in the great marketplace,

which presented the most magnificent appearance. All the houses which were round it were of filagreed sugar-work, with galleries towering above galleries; and in the centre stood a lofty cake covered with sugar, by way of obelisk, with fountains round it spouting orgeade, lemonade, and other delicious beverages into the air. The runnels at the sides of the footways were full of creams, which you might have ladled up with a spoon if you had chosen. But prettier than all this were the delightful little people who were crowding about everywhere by the thousand, shouting, laughing, playing, and singing, in short, producing all that jubilant uproar which Marie had heard from the distance. There were beautifully dressed ladies and gentlemen, Greeks and Armenians, Tyrolese and Jews, officers and soldiers, clergymen, shepherds, jack-puddings, in short, people of every conceivable kind to be found in the world.

"The tumult grew greater towards one of the corners; the people streamed asunder. For the Great Mogul happened to be passing along there in his palanquin, attended by three-and-ninety grandees of the realm, and seven hundred slaves. But it chanced that the Fishermen's Guild, about five hundred strong, were keeping a festival at the opposite corner of the place; and it was rather an unfortunate coincidence that the Grand Turk took it in his head just at this particular moment to go out for a ride, and crossed the square with three thousand Janissaries. And, as if this were not enough, the grand procession of the Interrupted Sacrifice came along at the same time, marching up towards the obelisk with a full orchestra playing, and the chorus singing:

Hail! all hail to the glorious sun!'

"So there was a thronging and a shoving, a driving and a squeaking; and soon lamentations arose, and cries of pain, for one of the fishermen had knocked a Brahmin's head off in the throng, and the Great Mogul had been very nearly run down by a jack-pudding. The din grew wilder and wilder. People were beginning to shove one another, and even to come to fisticuffs; when the man in the brocade dressing-gown who had welcomed Nutcracker as prince at the gate, clambered up to the top of the obelisk, and, after a very clear-tinkling bell had rung thrice, shouted, very loudly, three several times:

"Pastrycook! pastrycook! pastrycook!'

"Instantly the tumult subsided. Everybody tried to save his bacon as quickly as he could; and, after the entangled processions had been got disentangled, the dirt properly brushed off the Great Mogul, and the Brahmin's head stuck 011 again all right, the merry noise went on just the same as before.

Tell me why that gentleman called out "Pastrycook," Mr. Drosselmeier, please,' said Marie.

Ah! dearest Miss Stahlbaum,' said Nutcracker, 'in this place "Pastrycook" means a certain unknown and very terrible Power, which, it is believed, can do with people just what it chooses. It represents the Fate, or Destiny, which rules these happy little people, and they stand in such awe and terror of it that the mere mention of its name quells the wildest tumult in a moment, as the burgomaster has just shown.

Nobody thinks further of earthly matters, cuffs in the ribs, broken heads, or the like. Every one retires within himself, and says:

"What is man? and what his ultimate destiny?"'

"Marie could not forbear a cry of admiration and utmost astonishment as she now found herself all of a sudden before a castle, shining in roseate radiance, with a hundred beautiful towers. Here and there at intervals upon its walls were rich bouquets of violets, narcissus, tulips, carnations, whose dark, glowing colours heightened the dazzling whiteness, inclining to rose-colour, of the walls. The great dome of the central building, as well as the pyramidal roofs of the towers, were set all over with thousands of sparkling gold and silver stars.

Aha!' said Nutcracker, 'here we are at Marchpane Castle at last!'

"Marie was sunk and absorbed in contemplation of this magic palace. But the fact did not escape her that the roof was wanting to one of the principal towers, and that little men, up upon a scaffold made of sticks of cinnamon, were busy putting it on again. But before she had had time to ask Nutcracker about this, he said:

"This beautiful castle was a short time since threatened with tremendous havoc, if not with total destruction. Sweet-tooth the giant happened to be passing by, and he bit off the top of that tower there, and was beginning to gnaw at the great dome. But the Sweetmeatburgh people brought him a whole quarter of the town by way of tribute, and a considerable slice of Comfit Grove into the bargain. This stopped his mouth, and he went on his way.'

"At this moment soft, beautiful music was heard, and out came twelve little pages with lighted clove-sticks, which they held in their little hands by way of torches. Each of their heads was a pearl, their bodies were emeralds and rubies, and their feet were beautifully-worked pure gold. After them came four ladies about the size of Marie's Miss Clara, but so gloriously and brilliantly attired that Marie saw in a moment that they could be nothing but princesses of the blood royal. They embraced Nutcracker most tenderly, and shed tears of gladness, saying:

Oh, dearest prince! beloved brother!'

"Nutcracker seemed deeply affected. He wiped away his tears, which flowed thick and fast, and then he took Marie by the hand and said, with much pathos and solemnity:

"This is Miss Marie Stahlbaum, the daughter of a most worthy medical man, and the preserver of my life. Had she not thrown her slipper just in the nick of time--had she not procured me the pensioned Colonel's sword--I should have been lying in my cold grave at this moment, bitten to death by the accursed king of the mice. I ask you to tell me candidly, can Princess Pirlipat, princess though she be, compare for a moment with Miss Stahlbaum here in beauty, in goodness, in virtues of every kind? My answer is, emphatically "No."'

"All the ladies cried 'No,' and they fell upon Marie's neck with sobs and tears, and cried:

"Ah! noble preserver of our beloved royal brother! Excellent Miss Stahlbaum!'

"They now conducted Marie and Nutcracker into the castle, to a hall whose walls were composed of sparkling crystal. But what delighted Marie most of all was the furniture. There were the most darling little chairs, bureaus, writing-tables, and so forth, standing about everywhere, all made of cedar or Brazil-wood, covered with golden flowers. The princesses made Marie and Nutcracker sit down, and said that they would themselves prepare a banquet. So they went and brought quantities of little cups and dishes of the finest Japanese porcelain, and spoons, knives and forks, graters and stew-pans, and other kitchen utensils of gold and silver. Then they fetched the most delightful fruits and sugar things--such as Marie had never seen the like of--and began to squeeze the fruit in the daintiest way with their little hands, and to grate the spices and rub down the sugar-almonds; in short, they set to work so skilfully that Marie could see very well how accomplished they were in kitchen matters, and what a magnificent banquet there was going to be. Knowing her own skill in this line, she wished, in her secret heart, that she might be allowed to go and help the princesses, and have a finger in all these pies herself. And the prettiest of Nutcracker's sisters, just as if she had read the wishes of Marie's heart, handed her a little gold mortar, saying:

Sweet friend, dear preserver of my brother, would you mind just pounding a little of this sugar-candy?'

"Now as Marie went on pounding in the mortar with good will and the utmost enjoyment--and the sound of it was like a lovely song--Nutcracker began to relate, with much minuteness and prolixity, all that had happened on the occasion of the terrible engagement between his forces and the army of the king of the mice; how he had had the worst of it on account of the bad behaviour of his troops; how the horrible mouse king had all but bitten him to death, so that Marie had had to sacrifice a number of his subjects who were in her service, etc., etc.

"During all this it seemed to Marie as if what Nutcracker was saying--and even the sound of her own mortar--kept growing more and more indistinct, and going farther and farther away. Presently she saw a silver mistiness rising up all about, like clouds, in which the princesses, the pages, Nutcracker, and she herself were floating. And a curious singing and a buzzing and humming began, which seemed to die away in the distance; and then she seemed to be going up--up--up, as if on waves constantly rising and swelling higher and higher, higher and higher, higher and higher.

CONCLUSION.

"And then came a 'prr-poof,' and Marie fell down from some inconceivable height.

"That was a crash and a tumble!

"However, she opened her eyes, and, lo and behold, there she was in her own bed! It was broad daylight, and her mother was standing at her bedside, saying:

Well, what a sleep you have had! Breakfast has been ready for ever so long.'

"Of course, dear audience, you see how it was. Marie, confounded and amazed by all the wonderful things she had seen, had fallen asleep at last in Marchpane Castle, and the negroes or the pages, or perhaps the princesses themselves, had carried her home and put her to bed.

Oh, mother darling,' said Marie, what a number of places young Mr. Drosselmeier has taken me to in the night, and what beautiful things I have seen!' And she gave very much the same faithful account of it all as I have done to you.

"Her mother listened, looking at her with much astonishment, and, when she had finished, said:

You have had a long, beautiful dream, Marie; but now you must put it all out of your head.'

"Marie firmly maintained that she had not been dreaming at all; so her mother took her to the glass cupboard, lifted out Nutcracker from his usual position on the third shelf, and said:

You silly girl, how can you believe that this wooden figure

can have life and motion?'

Ah, mother,' answered Marie, 'I know perfectly well that Nutcracker is young Mr. Drosselmeier from Nürnberg, Godpapa Drosselmeier's nephew.'

"Her father and mother both burst out into ringing laughter.

It's all very well your laughing at poor Nutcracker, father,' cried Mary, almost weeping; 'but he spoke very highly of you; for when we arrived at Marchpane Castle, and he was introducing me to his sisters, the princesses, he said you were a most worthy medical man.'

The laughter grew louder, and Louise, and even Fritz, joined in it. Marie ran into the next room, took the mouse king's seven crowns from her little box, and handed them to her mother, saying:

"Look there, then, dear mother; those are the mouse king's seven crowns which young Mr. Drosselmeier gave me last night as a proof that he had got the victory.'

"Her mother gazed in amazement at the little crowns, which were made of some very brilliant, wholly unknown metal, and worked more beautifully than any human hands could have worked them. Dr. Stahlbaum could not cease looking at them with admiration and astonishment either, and both the father and the mother enjoined Marie most earnestly to tell them where she really had got them from. But she could only repeat what she had said before; and when her father scolded her, and accused her of untruthfulness, she began to cry bitterly, and said:

Oh, dear me; what can I tell you except the truth, poor unfortunate girl that I am!'

"At this moment the door opened, and Godpapa Drosselmeier came in, crying:

"'Hullo! hullo! what's all this? My little Marie crying? What's all this? what's all this?'

"Dr. Stahlbaum told him all about it, and showed him the crowns. As soon as he had looked at them, however, he cried out:

Stuff and nonsense! stuff and nonsense! These are the crowns I used to wear on my watch-chain. I gave them as a present to Marie on her second birthday. Do you mean to tell me you don't remember?'

"None of them did remember anything of the kind. But Marie, seeing that her father and mother's faces were clear of clouds again, ran up to her godpapa, crying:

You know all about the affair, Godpapa Drosselmeier; tell it to them then. Let them know from your own lips that my Nutcracker is your nephew, young Mr. Drosselmeier from Nürnberg, and that it was he who gave me the crowns.' But Drosselmeier made a very angry face, and muttered, 'Stupid stuff and nonsense!' upon which Marie's father took her in front of him, and said, with much earnestness:

Now just look here, Mario; let there be an end of all this foolish trash and absurd nonsense for once and for all; I'm not going to allow any more of it; and if ever I hear you say again that that idiotic, misshapen Nutcracker is your godpapa's nephew, I shall shy, not only Nutcracker, but all

93

your other playthings--Miss Clara not excepted--out of the window.'

"Of course poor Marie dared not utter another word concerning that which her whole mind was full of, for you may well suppose that it was impossible for anyone who had seen all that she had seen to forget it. And I regret to say that even Fritz himself at once turned his back on his sister whenever she wanted to talk to him about the wondrous realm in which she had been so happy. Indeed, he is said to have frequently murmured, 'Stupid goose!' between his teeth, though I can scarcely think this compatible with his proved kindness of heart. This much, however, is matter of certainty, that, as he no longer believed what his sister said, he now, on a public parade, formally recanted what he had said to his red hussars, and, in the place of the plumes he had deprived them of, gave them much taller and finer ones of goose quills, and allowed them to sound the march of the hussars of the guard as before.

"Marie did not dare to say anything more of her adventures. But the memories of that fairy realm haunted her with a sweet intoxication, and the music of that delightful, happy country still rang sweetly in her ears. Whenever she allowed her thoughts to dwell on all those glories she saw them again, and so it came about that, instead of playing as she used to do, she sat quiet and meditative, absorbed within herself. Everybody found fault with her for being this sort of little dreamer.

"It chanced one day that Godpapa Drosselmeier was

repairing one of the clocks in the house, and Marie was sitting beside the glass cupboard, sunk in her dreams and gazing at Nutcracker. All at once she said, as if involuntarily:

"Ah, dear Mr. Drosselmeier, if you really were alive, I shouldn't be like Princess Pirlipat, and despise you because you had had to give up being a nice handsome gentleman for my sake!'

Stupid stuff and nonsense!' cried Godpapa Drosselmeier.

"But, as he spoke, there came such a tremendous bang and shock that Marie fell from her chair insensible.

"When she came back to her senses her mother was busied about her and said:

"How could you go and tumble off your chair in that way, a big girl like you? Here is Godpapa Drosselmeier's nephew come from Nürnberg. See how good you can be.'

"Marie looked up. Her godpapa had got on his yellow coat and his glass wig, and was smiling in the highest good-humour. By the hand he was holding a very small but very handsome young gentleman. His little face was red and white; he had on a beautiful red coat trimmed with gold lace, white silk stockings and shoes, with a lovely bouquet of flowers in his shirt frill. He was beautifully frizzed and powdered, and had a magnificent queue hanging down his back. The little sword at his side seemed to be made entirely of jewels, it sparkled and shone so, and the little hat under his arm was woven of flocks of silk. He gave proof of the fineness of his manners in that he had brought for Marie a quantity of the most delightful toys--above all, the very same figures as those which the mouse king had eaten up--as well as a beautiful sabre for Fritz. He cracked nuts at table for the whole party; the very hardest did not withstand him. He placed them in his mouth with his left hand, tugged at his pigtail with his right, and crack! they fell in pieces.

"Marie grew red as a rose at the sight of this charming young gentleman; and she grew redder still when, after dinner, young Drosselmeier asked her to go with him to the glass cupboard in the sitting-room.

Play nicely together, children,' said Godpapa Drosselmeier; 'now that my clocks are all nicely in order, I can have no possible objection.'

"But as soon as young Drosselmeier was alone with Marie, he went down on one knee, and spake as follows:

Ah! my most dearly-beloved Miss Stahlbaum! 'see here at your feet the fortunate Drosselmeier, whose life you saved here on this very spot. You were kind enough to say, plainly and unmistakably, in so many words, that you would not have despised me, as Princess Pirlipat did, if I had been turned ugly for your sake. Immediately I ceased to be a contemptible Nutcracker, and resumed my former not altogether ill-looking person and form. Ah! most exquisite lady! bless me with your precious hand; share with me my crown and kingdom, and reign with me in Marchpane Castle, for there I now am king.'

"Marie raised him, and said gently:

Dear Mr. Drosselmeier, you are a kind, nice gentleman; and as you reign over a delightful country of charming, funny, pretty people, I accept your hand.'

"So then they were formally betrothed; and when a year and a day had come and gone, they say he came and fetched her away in a golden coach, drawn by silver horses. At the marriage there danced two-and-twenty thousand of the most beautiful dolls and other figures, all glittering in pearls and diamonds; and Marie is to this day the queen of a realm where all kinds of sparkling Christmas Woods, and transparent Marchpane Castles--in short, the most wonderful and beautiful things of every kind--are to be seen--by those who have the eyes to see them.

"So this is the end of the tale of Nutcracker and the King of the Mice."

"Tell me, dear Lothair," said Theodore, "how you can call your 'Nutcracker and the King of the Mice' a children's story? It is impossible that children should follow the delicate threads which run through the structure of it, and hold together its apparently heterogeneous parts. The most they could do would be to keep hold of detached fragments, and enjoy those, here and there."

"And is that not enough?" answered Lothair. "I think it is a great mistake to suppose that clever, imaginative children--and it is only they who are in question here--should content themselves with the empty nonsense which is so often set before them under the name of Children's Tales. They want something much better; and it is surprising how much they see and appreciate which escapes a good, honest, well-informed papa. Before I read this story to you, I read it to the only sort of audience whom I look upon as competent critics of it, to wit, my sister's children. Fritz, who is a great soldier, was delighted with his namesake's army, and the battle carried him away altogether. He cried 'prr and poof, and schmetterdeng, and boom booroom,' after me, in a ringing voice; jigged about on his chair, and cast an eye towards his sword, as if he would go to Nutcracker's aid when he got into danger. He had never read Shakespeare, or the recent newspaper accounts of fighting; so that all the significance of the military strategy and evolutions connected with that greatest of battles escaped him completely, as well as 'A horse! a horse! my kingdom for a horse!' And in the same way dear little Eugenie thoroughly appreciated, in her kind heart, Marie's regard for little Nutcracker, and was moved to tears when she sacrificed her playthings and her picture-books--even her little Christmas dress--to rescue her darling; and doubted not for a moment as to the existence of the glittering Candy Mead on to which Marie stepped from the neck of the mysterious fox-fur cloak in her father's wardrobe. The account of Toyland delighted the children more than I can tell."

"That part of your story," said Ottmar, "keeping in view the circumstance that the readers or listeners are to be children, I think the most successful. The interpolation of the story of the Hard Nut, although the 'cement' of the whole lies there, I consider to be a fault, because the story is--in appearance at all events--complicated and confused by it, and it rather stretches and broadens the threads. You have declared that we are incompetent critics, and so reduced us to silence; but I cannot help telling you that, if you bring this tale before the public, many very rational people--particularly those who never have been children themselves (which is the case with many)--will shrug their shoulders and shake their heads, and say the whole affair is a pack of stupid nonsense; or, at all events, that some attack of fever must have suggested your ideas, because nobody in his sound and sober senses could have written such a piece of chaotic monstrosity."

"Very good," said Lothair, "to such a head-shaker I should make a profound reverence, lay my hand on my heart, and assure him that it is little service to an author if all sorts of fancies dawn upon him in a confused dream, unless he can discuss them with himself by the light of sound reason and judgment, and work out the threads of them firmly and soberly. Moreover, I would say that no description of work demands a clear and quiet mind more absolutely than just this; for, although it must have the effect of flashing out in all directions with the most arbitrary disregard of all rules, it must contain a firm kernel within it."

"Nobody can gainsay you in this," said Cyprian. "Still, it must always be a risky undertaking to bring the utterly fanciful into the domain of everyday life, and clap mad, enchanted caps on to the heads of grave and sober folks--judges, students, and Masters of the Rolls--so that they go gliding about like ghosts in broad daylight up and down the most frequented streets of the most familiar towns, and one does not know what to think of his most respectable neighbours. It is true that this brings with it a certain tone of irony, which acts as a spur to the lazy spirit, or rather entices it, unobservedly, with a plausible face, into this unaccustomed province."

"But the said tone of irony," said Theodore, "is capable of becoming a most dangerous pitfall; for the pleasantness of the plot and execution--which we have a right to demand in all tales of the kind--may very easily trip over it and go tumbling to the bottom."

"But I do not believe it is possible to lay down definite canons for the construction of stories of this kind," said Lothair. "Tieck, the profound and glorious master--the creator of the most delightful works of the 'tale' class--has only placed a very few scattered, instructive hints on the subject in the mouths of the characters in his 'Phantasus.' According to them, the conditions are, a quietly progressive tone of the narrative; a certain guilelessness in the relation, which, like gently fantasising music, enters the soul without noise or din. There should be no bitter after-taste left behind by it, but only a sense of enjoyment, echoing on. But is this sufficient to define the only admissible tone for this species of literature? However, I don't wish to think any more about my 'Nutcracker.' I feel that it is pervaded by what I may call 'overflowing spirits' to too great an extent; and I have thought too much of grown-up people and their ways and doings; for the rest, I have had to promise the little critics in my sister's nursery to get another story ready for them by next Christmas, and I undertake to keep it in a quieter tone. For to-day, I think we ought to be thankful that I have summoned you up out of the dreadful mine-shaft at Falun to the light of day, and restored you to the good humour and good spirits which become Serapion Brethren--particularly at the moment of parting, for I hear the clock striking twelve."

"May Serapion continue to protect and aid us," cried Theodore, rising and elevating his glass, "and enable us to describe what we have seen with the eye of the spirit, in graphic and apposite words."

The Brethren drank the toast, and parted.

Made in the USA
Middletown, DE
10 October 2016